'We're going home in ~~Sep~~ ~~...~~ :y at last.'

'How long a visit?' I could never understand why everyone called the UK home; home for me was here, our farm in Shillong.

'Bernard and I will stay for a couple of months, but you—' My mother stopped; she didn't meet my eye.

'You're not leaving me behind—'

'It's time we started to take your education seriously.'

I stared at her. I felt as if I was being sucked into a nightmare, unable to shout for help while huge and horrible things moved towards me to crush me . . .

OUT OF THE SUN

PEGGY WOODFORD

Although this book has grown out of the author's own childhood experiences in Assam and Guernsey, the characters are mainly imaginary and so are some of the background details.

OUT OF THE SUN
A CORGI FREEWAY BOOK 0 552 526541

First published in Great Britain by
Macmillan Children's Books

PRINTING HISTORY
Macmillan edition published 1990
Corgi Freeway edition published 1991

This book is set in 11pt Palatino by
Kestrel Data, Exeter

Corgi Freeway Books are published by Transworld Publishers Ltd, 61-63 Uxbridge Road, Ealing, London W5 5SA, in Australia by Transworld Publishers (Australia) Pty Ltd, 15-23 Helles Avenue, Moorebank, NSW 2170, and in New Zealand by Transworld Publishers (NZ) Ltd, Cnr Moselle and Waipareira Avenues, Henderson, Auckland.

Made and printed in Great Britain by
Cox & Wyman Ltd, Reading, Berks.

For Walter

ASSAM
1947

Icing sugar peaks – Chen, Chumo, Kangdu, Nyegi Kainsang – rise above the lower ranks of mountains, sometimes blue, sometimes pink, rarely pure white. Chen, Chumo, Kangdu, Nyegi Kainsang. Each one is over 22,000 feet but from where I stand on the Shillong Peak, gazing across at the far distant Himalayas, they look tiny, pretty, unreal. I dream about those mountains; one day I'll go trekking there.

'Go to Bhutan, it's the nearest thing to paradise you'll find in this world,' I heard someone say to my father, and ever since then I've longed to go to one of those high Himalayan states, Bhutan or Sikkim or Nepal. Next year we'll go, says my father, always next year. Not that I need to go anywhere to find paradise; I have it already.

Icing sugar mountains, far across the Assam Valley, Chen, Chumo, Kangdu, Nyegi Kainsang . . .

1

'We're going home in September, Nancy. Guernsey at last.'

'How long a visit?' I could never understand why everyone called the UK home; home for me was here, our farm in Shillong.

'Bernard and I will stay for a couple of months, but you—' My mother stopped; she didn't meet my eye.

'You're not leaving me behind—'

'It's time we started to take your education seriously.'

I stared at her. I felt as if I was being sucked into a nightmare, unable to shout for help while huge and horrible things moved towards me to crush me.

'You must try and understand why it's for the best. I know we've always said we wouldn't leave you on your own in England as other parents do, but things have changed. The war lasted much longer than anyone expected and now that your father's been offered an extra two years to help the Indians get used to Independence—'

'I heard Dad say we were all here until 1949, *surely* he meant me as well.'

My mother tried to put her arm around me, but I pulled myself away. The nightmare began to recede; I was certain I could persuade my parents to let me stay if they were staying. I wasn't ready to be ripped from paradise yet.

'Aunt Sophie has spoken to the headmistress at

the college and she insists that this year when you're rising fourteen is the last sensible time to move you; if we wait until you're nearly sixteen you'll never catch up.'

'Pinemount School is fine—'

'No it's not and you know it. You must start working for your School Certificate and you can't possibly do that here.'

'School isn't everything. *Please* let me come back with you.' I wanted to shake my mother, to grab her by the hair, the ears, to make her see that I couldn't be left in Guernsey to live with my unknown relations. 'You won't leave Clare behind, will you?'

'Of course not. She's far too young.' At that very moment my little sister Clare came in on her chubby legs and held her hands up.

'Ma-ma,' she said, just like a talking doll. As my mother picked her up I felt my desperation transfer itself to Clare. I wanted to scratch her pretty baby face and tear out those golden curls. I watched her poke her fingers into Mum's nose and gurgle. 'Mama.' Horrible lucky Clare.

'What you don't realize is how much you're going to enjoy a new life in Guernsey. You've been far too much on your own here. You've had no chance to get to know enough people your own age.'

'Two more years. Please let me come back with you, Mum. Please. I love India so much I can't bear the thought of leaving it.'

'In that case two more years won't make a lot of difference.'

'Yes, they will. I'm bound to change, particularly

9

if I've been home on leave.' I felt this was a masterly point, but my mother just sighed.

'Nancy, be reasonable. The last thing we want to do is be parted from you but your education is all-important now . . .'

'Ma-ma.' Clare put her arms round Mum's neck in a strangling hug. I couldn't stand being near the two of them any longer, so I ran out of the house.

'Nancy. *Nancy!* Come back!'

I rushed across the wide lawn towards the mimosa trees that bordered our garden. When in flower, they were a mass of heady-scented tiny yellow pompoms, but now they were a sombre grey-green row, keeping out the jungle. Automatically I headed for my tree-house, even though I hardly ever use it now. No-one had a tree-house like mine; our *mistri* – carpenter – Bahyong built it for my eighth birthday and he and I spent the next two years improving it. It was in a particularly large mimosa tree and had a wooden staircase up to the front door and a rope ladder up to the back.

It had two windows, with glass panes, and a thatched roof like the roof of our bungalow. I could stand up inside it. There was a scaled-down table and chairs and a dresser with odd bits of china in it. The floor was covered with bamboo matting. It smelled of tropical woods and bamboo and the jungle outside; it was the most wonderful tree-house. Even though I'd grown too old for it I still loved it dearly. I only went there to be on my own or to escape people I didn't know who'd come to visit my parents. I carried Clare up the other day and made a little tea party for her. She loved it and

10

cried when Congreeal, our *ayah* or nanny, came to take her away at her bedtime.

Laughing and Rinjo were Congreeal's children. They were Khasis, an Assamese tribe, and had been my good friends ever since Congreeal joined us seven years ago. Laughing's name was typical among the Khasis; they took any European word they liked the sound of for a Christian name. There was a famous trio of sisters called Million, Billion and Trillion. Laughing was exactly my age but she looked years older. She'd got an almost adult figure and wore lots of jewellery and told me she was going to get married soon. Rinjo was eleven; he was amazing at imitating animal and bird noises. He had pop eyes and big toes that stuck up and he made me laugh. They couldn't speak English so we talked to each other in Khasi. My mother got a bit worried sometimes about my friendship with Laughing and Rinjo, mainly because she couldn't understand very much of what we were saying. I don't think she would have approved that long ago they explained the facts of life to me; they described how babies were made and we inspected each other down there and had a good talk. Then the subject was dropped and we haven't mentioned it since.

As I ran towards the tree-house, I saw Rinjo in the distance. I didn't want to talk to him, I didn't want to talk to anyone, so I kept my head down until I jumped on to the wooden staircase leading up to the front door. There was a loud cracking noise and the whole staircase collapsed. Essential struts had rotted; I rubbed my bruised shins and went up the back ladder instead. I unlatched the back door and swung myself in; it had been ages

11

since my last visit. The place smelled musty and as I opened a window I looked round for intruders: snakes or insects. A few ants and a large spider were all I could see and a huddle of stink bugs minding their own business, so I left them all alone. Luckily insects don't bother me, which is just as well. Anyone who gets fussed about creepy-crawlies has a rotten time in India. I think the only ones that give me nightmares are the elephant leeches; I'm not madly keen on ordinary leeches, which come looping towards you from all sides if you stand still on a jungle path, but I know that they'll drop off the moment you touch them with a lighted cigarette or match. Elephant leeches live in water and they are horrid. My father was once trapped in a pool of water when his car ran off the road and he says if he hadn't been rescued quickly, he would surely have died from loss of blood; huge leeches covered his body.

Guernsey. No elephant leeches, no stink bugs, but what did I care. I didn't want to leave India yet. I wasn't ready to. I hadn't been to Kashmir, I hadn't seen the Taj Mahal, but most important I hadn't trekked up into the Himalayas. As I sat in that little tree-house, rather big for it now, my love for India was like a pain.

'Nancy! Tea!' I could hear my mother calling. I didn't answer. I saw her standing indecisively in the middle of the lawn, looking towards the tree-house. Then Congreeal appeared with Clare in her arms; Clare was eating a biscuit which she accidentally dropped. Fuss, our Jack Russell, was on to it in a trice and as he chewed it up triumphantly Clare started to wail. Everyone went back inside to give

Clare cuddles and more biscuits. I whistled to Fuss who trotted over to the base of the mimosa tree; I wanted him to come up but of course the stairs were broken. He sat whining below me and I put my head on the tree-house table and cried.

2

I suppose some children might have been lonely in my situation. Our house was five miles out of the hill station of Shillong and there were no Europeans near us and not that many now in Shillong itself. But from when I was tiny I'd got used to amusing myself and there were plenty of people around to talk to if I felt like it. Right from the beginning I was brought up to be trilingual, so I now spoke fluent Khasi and Hindustani, much better than my mother though not as well as my father who of course had had to learn both for his work.

My father, Bernard Sykes, was Director of Agiculture for Assam. We lived on a special farm; nearby were acres and acres of fields full of experimental crops and breeds of livestock. Dad tried to introduce Rhode Island Red chickens and Merino sheep from Australia. Their chicks and lambs were gorgeous – I went to see them as often as I could. I was allowed to keep a lamb as a pet; I called her Jemima and she followed me around. Now she's full-grown she's gone back to the flock, but whenever I go near her and call she comes running, her huge woolly body like a sausage above her thin legs.

Our house, like all the houses in Shillong, was

built to withstand the frequent earthquakes, mostly little tremors as if the ground was shaking itself gently as a dog shakes itself when it's wet. Our house was made of dark-coloured wood and white plaster; it had lots of windows and a deep veranda all round it, and a thatched roof that was alive with birds and little animals. I loved the noise they all made in the evenings and the early mornings, chattering and twittering and running over the canvas ceilings with pattering feet. All local houses were also built on stilts and snakes liked living under them. We'd never found one, but Fuss got hysterical sometimes as he ferreted underneath.

We lived on our verandas; they were deep and cool and airy. There were flowers everywhere, creeping up the struts, spilling out of tubs and pots all along the edges of the verandas and down the steps. I could look out from my bedroom and see and smell nothing but flowers. I would lie in bed and wait for the flap flap of Congreeal's bare feet as she came along the veranda with my early breakfast: fruit juice – orange, papaya, mango – and a sliced banana.

'Morning time, Missy-baba Nancy. Morning time.' She spoke English with a Welsh accent because she'd been taught at the Welsh Mission. Usually we spoke Khasi, but there were times of the day when she liked to use her English. She would lift the mosquito net out of the way and give her lovely warm smile. She was pale-skinned like all Khasis and her eyes were slightly Chinese; she smelled of clean sari and betel-nut and rice. I loved her dearly. Everyone said she spoiled me, but as far as I was concerned she was perfect; we were comfortable together. She sang me Khasi songs in her nasal voice and told me stories about the snakes the Khasis worshipped. Important Khasi families had their own snakes, called *Thlem*, and these were supposed to bring prosperity to the owners. Sometimes, Congreeal whispered, these holy snakes needed to be offered sacrifices and human blood was shed. Congreeal's family was too poor to have its own snake; if they wanted to worship a snake, they had to go to the head family in their village.

My father told me that the Khasi language was like no other in India and that the tribe came long ago from Mongolia, which was why they had slanted eyes and flat faces. Laughing had eyes like slits. She could spit betel-nut juice further than anyone on our compound: the arc of bright pink juice travelled yards. I used to try to copy her, but mine just went a boring little distance. Rinjo and I used to sit in the tree-house chewing betel-nut and practising our spitting. Mum got furious if she found out; she forbade me to chew betel. Not that I much liked the taste; it was spitting that pink juice I enjoyed.

3

We had lots of servants because it was expected of us – the Indians made sure that Europeans employed as many of them as possible. Since my father was Director of Agriculture, he was a boss, a burra-sahib – *burra* means big – and he had to live in the proper style whether he liked it or not. So, beginning at the lowliest, we had a sweeper to clean the floors inside and the paths outside and to empty chamber pots and the thunderboxes – we had no main sewerage. He was an Untouchable, the lowest caste of Hindu. He sang in a high-pitched whine as he worked; first he would sweep the paths round the house in the very early morning, so we always woke up to the gentle swish swish of his besom and his weird chanting. He had a huge white beard and was known as Happy.

We had two *malis* or gardeners, Gopal and his son Ram; we had a *dhobi* or washerman called Guru who was also the water-carrier or *pani-wallah* because of course everything had to be done by hand; there was no electricity or running water so all our clothes were washed by Guru in a river. Our bath water was heated and brought to the *gussul-khana* or bathroom by Guru; the heavy cans of steaming water were suspended from a yoke across his shoulders and we would always know bathtime was near when we heard the great clank as the cans hit the concrete floor.

'*Gussul pani gurum!*' he'd shout as he poured it, hot and steaming, into the tin bath. Crash, clank, clang.

We had a cook, a Christian from Goa called John, we had a Muslim bearer called Abdul who ran the house and did all the organising and shopping under my mother's close supervision, as well as serving us at table and handing round drinks if we had guests. Abdul was very tall and stately and looked down on all the other servants. But he had two wives who were always fighting and spoiling his reputation in the servants' *godowns* – little houses

16

at the edge of our property – so respect for him ended the moment he stepped out of our garden. He loved going on tour with Dad; once a month they would go off and he'd escape from his wives.

We had two *syces* or grooms who actually lived in the stables, over the horses, by choice. Since the stables were one of my favourite places, I got to know Purram Das and his assistant syce very well. We had four horses, all country bred or 'tats' which were cheap to buy and cheap to keep in India. People who would never dream of keeping a horse in England were able to have several. I'd been given a horse of my own when I was seven which I called Why Not because her ears were the shape of question marks. I loved her, how I loved her. She was full of fun, she would flick her ears at me and snort and her eyes would say, 'Where's my sugar cane' so clearly I felt I'd heard the words. I'd have the piece of sugar cane behind my back and she'd try and nudge me to turn round. She was terribly greedy and had a lovely round belly. Purram Das loved her too; she was his favourite, though he'd often swear at her when she nipped his bottom if he stopped grooming her when, in her opinion, he hadn't finished. *'Ari! Shaitan!'* All the horses adored being groomed; Indian syces do it by hand. They call it *hart molesh* which just means hand-rubbing in Hindi and it's fascinating to watch. They use the whole of their hands and forearms to beat out the dust and dead hair, slap slap slap, and the horses grunt with pleasure. Then they put leather pads like home-made boxing gloves on their hands and go on beating out the dust and sweat, first the right pad, then the left then the two together. You could hear their rhythmic beating up at the house: thump, thump, THUMP. Both syces would do it, keeping in time with each other. I'd tried to do it and failed dismally. I couldn't keep up the rhythm at all and found it very hard work. Why Not clearly didn't approve of my efforts.

We also had two servants we shared with the foreman down on the farm: there was Bahyong the mistri who'd built me my tree-house and who made most of our furniture and toys, and there was Ahmed the dirzi who made and mended all our clothes. When Ahmed came he sat cross-legged on the veranda, turning the old Singer sewing machine at great speed with one hand. He'd often hold the material steady with his big toe and first toe. When I was little I tried to do this too, but my toes got tired after a few seconds. Ahmed laughed his wheezy laugh and said without agile toes I'd never make a dirzi – I told Rinjo he'd make a good dirzi with his enormous big toes, but he ignored me; he wants to be a syce. Ahmed had a big fat pin-cushion made of red fabric, stuffed hard; stuck full of pins it looked like a strange spiky fruit. Ahmed used to make lovely neat doll's clothes for me out of dress scraps; my doll was called Heather and for a long time I thought of her as a real person. I wanted to dress her in a sari and choli, the little blouse that went with it, but Ahmed didn't approve. Heather was a white doll belonging to a 'missy baba'. No sari. But to make up he used to bring me Indian sweetmeats – he knew how much I adored these – and for some reason my mother didn't really like me eating them. So it was a secret between him and me; I used to run down the drive to meet him and if he had any sweetmeats for me, he'd slip them over then and I'd hide them in my tree-house and eat them at intervals during the day. My favourites were jalebis, which were golden crisp spirals filled with honey-like syrup. I liked sandesh too, a fudge made from curd cheese and pistachio and cardamoms and lime juice. And the great treat was tiltandula, a sort of solid meringue tasting strongly of sesame seeds. Ahmed told me the secret of the wonderful flavour of tiltandula was a pinch of ground wood . . . sandalwood.

'They're all so terribly sweet and scented' I once heard Mum say when she'd been offered sweet-meats at some Indian house in Shillong. 'No wonder all those women were so fat.' I kept so quiet about my supply of sweetmeats that she never guessed how often I ate them and at least they didn't make me fat.

I loved Ahmed, but I loved our mistri, Bahyong, even more. He was a Khasi, small, bandy-legged and full of smiles. He had hardly any teeth, but the few he had he managed to whistle through. Our sweeper, Happy, was always singing his wailing song and Bahyong was always whistling. Dad said it was like having a pair of human musical kettles in the garden.

Bahyong was the most patient person I knew. All we Sykes are very impatient as a family; we get in a bait over the smallest things. But Bahyong would sit for hours trying to make one piece of wood dovetail perfectly with another and even sanded and finished, to a marvellous standard, the furniture for my tree-house. Nothing would make him cut corners. He said he got no pleasure from *kutcha* work. Somebody gave me a doll's wardrobe and the door fell off almost immediately. Bahyong wouldn't mend it; he said the toy was too kutcha to repair. Nothing I said would persuade him to put the new hinges on so I fixed them myself with glue and broken pins from Ahmed's cushion.

'*Kutcha*,' said Bahyong when he saw what I'd done. '*Kutcha*.'

4

'Nancy, we must sort through your old toys. Most of them will do for Clare, but there may be some we don't want to keep and of course you'll want to take some with you.'

'I don't want to take any on leave.' My mother sighed.

'Do you want me to sort through them and do as I think fit—'

'I don't want Clare to have Heather. She's too young, she'll break Heather to bits.'

'Well then, take Heather with you, or Clare might be tempted to play with her later on.'

'You don't really and truly mean to leave me in Guernsey when I'm so against it. Please, Mum, please, please, please don't leave me there.'

'Nancy, I can't understand you. You're being so utterly negative about your life. You don't want this, you don't want that. You can't stop life changing, you can't arrest the passage of time . . .'

'Clare can have Heather, she can have all my old toys.'

'I wasn't talking about Heather and you know it. Heather is yours to do what you like with. I was talking about your attitude to your future . . .'

All around me were heaps of toys . . . my grey stuffed elephant on wheels, my old teddy, a gollywog, a clown, heaps of old blocks and bricks and painted Indian soldiers, and of course Heather and her wardrobe, cot, wooden pram and goodness knows what else. I looked at Heather's simpering face and shiny round cheeks and suddenly couldn't stand her any longer. All my childhood lay there and Heather's silly expression seemed to mock it. My mother was nattering on about my future but I felt at that moment that my past was being torn away, my special past that made me what I was. Something went snap inside me; I leaped at Heather and threw her hard against the wall. There was an untidy cracking noise and she fell to pieces. Her head, arms and legs flew off and her poor body dropped with an empty clatter on the wooden floor.

There was a terrible silence. My mother started rubbing her face with her hands, a thing she does when she's upset. I was shaking; I felt slightly sick. Heather's head lay near my feet, her long-lashed lids covering her bright blue eyes.

'Oh, Nancy,' whispered Mum.

I was on the point of bursting into tears and throwing myself into her arms when the playroom door swung open and Clare waddled in. Congreeal had just got her up from her rest. She beamed at us and then picked up one of Heather's legs and her body. She bumped down on her nappied bottom and started trying to fit the two together by putting the leg into the neck hole. Mum gave a strangled noise and swooped her up in a bear hug; I was left standing there, dying for a hug myself but unable to move.

5

Icing sugar mountains, far across the Assam Valley, Chen, Chumo, Kangdu, Nyegi Kainsang. Every time I rode Why Not up to the top of the Shillong Peak, I looked across at them. I waited for my father to say that we were going to put everything aside and go trekking up into those magical-sounding countries, Bhutan or Nepal or Sikkim. It was the only thing that would make leaving India for good bearable . . .

'I know what Nancy would really like to do.' I gazed at my father in wild hope. 'Camp at Horseshoe Falls. What's the matter, Nancy, I thought it was your favourite place on earth and you've always wanted to camp there?'

'Of course I do. I just wondered . . . are we going to go on a longer tour or anything?'

'There's no time before we leave. I've got a ludicrous amount to do still and there are only four weeks left before that ship sails. But this week-end I am determined to take my Nancy somewhere I know she loves. Tell you what, Helen, why don't we invite the Allotsons as well. Give Nancy a chance to see Bruce again.' I knew he had been about to say for the last time instead of again. 'Wouldn't you like that?'

'Yes.' I smiled. I *was* pleased, but it was like

getting one little Christmas present when you'd been half-expecting a pony or a bike.

Four weeks. Only four weeks before I had to leave the place where I had spent the whole of my blissful life – blissful that is until I'd been told I'd be losing it. There's something awful about doing things that may be for the last time. Or seeing things: Bahyong told me there was a group of elephants being walked past our gate. I ran down the long drive, in time to see the end of a line of *hathi* plodding slowly away. Assam still had lots of elephants and hundreds of them would be rounded up each year and trained and then walked down to the great elephant fairs on the plains. I had been fascinated by elephants ever since my father had once taken us to Nowgong on tour, to watch an elephant catch. A special viewing platform had been built near the stockade and we went up into it at night to see the wild elephants brought in. Driven along by the hunters with drum beats and wild shouting, the poor animals suddenly found themselves surrounded by a stockade. They trumpeted and banged their heads against the wooden palings and I began to cry. It seemed so cruel to deprive them of their freedom. Dad told me that the elephant population of Assam was so large that it could stand two or three hundred being removed every year and that besides, elephant catching was such an important business and provided so many people with work and pay that to ban it would have been politically impossible. But it still hurt to see them all confused and desperate and I was thrilled when the next day they managed to break through the stockade and escape. One very big male had banged

23

and banged until the gates had collapsed. So now whenever I saw a line of them being taken anywhere I always willed them to escape. But I knew they were tamed and had got attached to their mahouts or riders, and it was unlikely they'd ever escape. One that actually did, met its mahout in the wild after years of freedom and when the man commanded it to *bait* – sit – down sat the elephant and the man got on its back and brought it home.

So I watched from the end of the drive until the last grey wrinkled rear with its twitching tail and strangely-articulated legs and feet disappeared from sight. I might never see an Indian elephant again, except in some nasty English zoo. I could smell elephant droppings at the mouth of our drive. What a long walk the poor things had ahead of them, right to the plains of Central India.

6

Shillong was surrounded by waterfalls, as small rivers plunged down from the high plateau into deep gorges and joined the main river, the Umniam. (*Um* was the Khasi word for river, so all the rivers and streams were called *um*-something. I always thought *um* was a very watery word, just right for what it meant.) There were the Spreadeagle Falls, the Crinoline Falls, the Elephant Falls, the Beadon Falls, the Sweet Falls. Like roaring creamy glass the water poured down, poured and poured without any change so that from a distance it really did look static and solid, like glass. I loved the way they never stopped and yet looked the same. It was hypnotic. I could see exactly why people wanted to throw themselves into waterfalls to see what would happen.

The Horseshoe Falls were different from the others; only twenty to thirty feet high instead of hundreds. They were further out of Shillong, too, and no-one but us ever went there. We'd christened them Horseshoe Falls because of their shape. They were too small to be on any map.

The setting was perfect. There were pine-woods all round, full of green rides, and a small gorge nearby overhung with creeper-covered trees; if you detached a creeper it made a wonderful swing. Out you swung over the thick jungle in the gorge. My father always tested the creepers with his full weight before he let us use them.

At the base of the falls was a horseshoe-shaped pool; the main body of water rushed away to the right, but at the quiet end of the horseshoe was a little pebble beach where it was safe to swim. There were large grey boulders in the water like bathing elephants, a family of hathi I called them when I was little, and certainly there was a big boar hathi and a smaller mother and fleet of young ones. All that was missing was trunks and tails.

How we loved that spot. We built our own fireplace out of small grey stones all carefully fitted together and it stayed undisturbed from one year to the next. Abdul had inserted pieces of metal so that he could cook a whole meal on it. But usually we went without him and boiled our own water and fried eggs and grilled meat and chapatis. I had nagged my parents for years to camp there, but since

Dad had to camp all the time when he went on tour for his job, he didn't regard camping as holiday fun. So for him to suggest that we did so showed what an effort he was making.

'Such a lot of trouble just for one night,' murmured my mother.

'Nonsense. Abdul will organize everything. He loves getting away from those two wives, he'll be delighted. He can bring everything in the car and we can take the pony-trap.' My father clapped his hands together and then flicked me lightly on the cheek. 'Who's happy now?'

'How can I be happy when I know this is for the last time.'

'Just live for the moment. Don't use words like "ever" and "last" and "never". Just live for the moment, Nancy.'

It may have been good advice, but it was difficult to follow. The words 'ever' and 'never' and 'last' seemed impossible to banish. When I went to the tree-house to cry, I found Bahyong banging away, mending the broken staircase. He stopped whistling to grin at me.

'Soon finished, Missy-baba, soon finished. Good as new.'

'What's the point of mending it, Bahyong. I won't be here to use it and Clare will be too young.' His eyes dropped as he rubbed the new handrail with sandpaper.

'Very fortunate to go home to UK,' he murmured.

'I don't think so. I want to stay here for two more years, until the *Sahib* retires for good.' Bahyong rubbed industriously. As usual, he was going to

26

work at this useless staircase until it was perfect, whatever I said. 'Two more years. What's wrong with that?'

'All English children go home for education. You must go too.'

I stared at him depressed; I'd expected sympathy from him. A sudden rush of annoyance filled me.

'Anyway, what's the point of wasting your time mending that stupid staircase? Let it rot.' Bahyong flashed a look at me; I couldn't tell what he was thinking.

'Memsahib asked me to mend it.' He finished rubbing the handrail and ran his hands over it to check its smoothness. There was a lovely smell of fresh pine-wood. 'Now I prime it. Come, Missy-baba Nancy, come to the workshop. Ahmed has sent you jalebis. I have them in the workshop.' Bahyong picked up his bag of tools and led the way to the lean-to behind the garage. I followed his thin figure in its old jacket and dhoti.

'Do you know, Bahyong, I think I'm taller than you now.'

'We measure.' He put me against the workshop door. 'Five feet two inches. Bahyong is five feet one inches. You will be tall one day, tall like the Sahib.' His measuring tape zipped back into its metal and leather container when he pressed a button. Mum had given him this measure; it was his most fiercely-guarded possession. He put it into an inner pocket of his tattered jacket. I suddenly wanted to hug him and cry at the same time, but he'd already turned away and was looking for a paint brush and his primer. Then he handed me a little basket in which there were three golden crispy twirls full of sweetness and set off back to the tree-house. I wasn't going to follow, but he motioned me to do so.

'Missy-baba try the staircase please.'

So I climbed up the new staircase and sat in the dear little room and looked out of the window down on to Bahyong's busy head. I offered him a jalebi but he refused; I ate all three while he whistled away through his teeth and neatly primed the new wood, my heart full of love for him.

7

Why Not sensed something was wrong in my life. She twitched her question-mark ears and behaved oddly. Purram Das told me she was off her food, though she always loved any treats of sugar cane or carrots that I brought her. She actually threw me one morning. We were out for the morning ride and she suddenly decided she'd out-gallop my parents' two horses, Amazon and Pempa, and took off towards Shillong Peak at a mad pace. I could hear my parents shouting as they raced after me, but above the thudding hooves I couldn't hear what they were saying. I hung on grimly for as long as I could, until Why Not did an unexpected swerve round a fallen pine-tree and I sailed off as if I'd been catapulted. Luckily I landed in the thickest branches of the fallen pine, which cushioned my fall.

'That was a terrific bit of riding,' said my father when he rode up. 'I don't know how you managed to stay on as long as you did.'

Why Not had galloped off, no doubt already on

her way back home. I could picture her smug expression and Purram Das's horror as she returned, riderless.

I rode again next morning, but this time Dad had Why Not on a leading rein in case. I didn't mind; I was still feeling very sore and a bit nervous to start with. But Why Not was being so placid that I think she was trying to say sorry. And to be honest I was glad to go slowly for once, because since I'd been allowed to ride on a par with Mum and Dad I'd had to work hard in order to keep up.

Nothing, but nothing was better than the early morning in India: the air was soft and clear and sweet-smelling before the heat of the day; there were smudges of mist in the distance and twinkles of dew on every leaf. Everyone on the farm was up; it was a time for cleansing and purification and prayer. The Hindus would ritually wash themselves as they faced the rising sun; the Muslims were bent over on their prayer mats before the sun even came up. The Buddhist prayer wheels whirled in the light morning breeze. John the Goan cook said his rosary loudly, alone in the kitchen.

As we left, our sweeper began to sweep the verandas with a broom made of soft grass; later he'd use a besom of scratchy twigs on the paths. Swish, swish, scratch, swish. Our tame myna bird shouted 'hullo, hullo, hullo' endlessly and whistled at the wild birds who came near. Our horses crunched down the drive and then we aimed for one of the dozens of beautiful rides in our area.

'Where would you like to go today?' Dad asked me. It was a particularly clear day for the onset of the rainy season and so I said the Peak, the view would be so good today; soon it would be obscured by mist and distant rain as July moved towards August. The Peak was over six thousand feet above sea-level and on a clear day, like that one, you could see a huge tract of country all round, an area one hundred miles across. In the north were the peaks of the Himalayas of Bhutan, in front of them was the valley of the great Brahmaputra River, a silver snake on the valley floor. The Brahmaputra: a huge, strange river that rose in Tibet and started by flowing east for three hundred miles, cut through the Himalayas into Assam and turned round and flowed west for another two hundred and fifty miles before it turned south and joined the Ganges.

There were ranges of hills all round us, the Naga Hills, the Lushai Hills, the Garo Hills. Lots of tribes lived in the jungles on their slopes: my father said that some were still emerging from the Iron Age, they were so primitive. They wore artificial tails and collected human heads as trophies . . . Stories about them made me shiver and used to give me nightmares.

Today the peaks of the Himalayas weren't like icing sugar; they were grey-white in the morning sun, like a row of small sharp teeth.

'You said we would go trekking in the Himalayas one day.'

'I know I did. It's something I've dreamed of all my years in India.' My father rode beside me, holding Why Not's leading rein. Mum had galloped on ahead.

'Then why haven't you been?'

'Time has passed and I haven't got myself

30

organized. Silly reasons. But you'll find that life is ruled by silly reasons.'

'Do you think you'll get there in the next two years?'

'I doubt it, Nancy. Apart from anything, I'll have used up all my leave taking you home.'

'Do I really have to stay behind in Guernsey, Dad?'

I hadn't meant to say it, I'd given up hope, but as the words came out I was glad I'd tried once more. There was a pause, broken only by the sound of squeaking leather harness and the clunks as Why Not chewed the bit.

'Nancy, I wish I could be as sure as Helen that it's the right thing to do. I always said I would never send my children home while I still worked in India, because it seemed so cruel. But then I didn't expect to stay on after Independence and so you're older than I'd bargained for. You need your education. It's only two years, Nancy, only two. In the old days children went home at five and six and were separated from their parents on and off for the rest of their childhood. Two years will flash past.'

'Since it's such a short time I can't see it makes any difference whether I come back or stay. After all, I can catch up with my education later.' Hope was beginning to rise in me, my father sounded so undecided. 'I love my life here so much, Dad. No-one could have had a better childhood than me.'

'You're unusual, Nancy, you know. Most children wouldn't see their lives so clearly.'

'I can't help it. Being told I have to leave all this has made me think. I'll just wither away in Guernsey.'

'Don't be ridiculous. You're going to have to live there in the end, after all.'

'I'll accept then. We'll all have to.' I'd been longing to talk like this with one of my parents, but somehow my mother just wouldn't let me get going. I remained a little girl with her and said stupid things.

'I'll talk to your mother. But nothing is likely to change, you know. Too much has been arranged, Nancy; you've got a place at the college; Sophie's been very energetic on your behalf.'

'We could just put the place off for two years.'

'You're a persistent little devil.'

Ahead of us, my mother was waiting as Amazon paced restlessly about.

'You're both looking very serious,' she said as we drew level.

'It's nothing,' I began.

'Nancy has almost persuaded me that it would be wrong to leave her in Guernsey.' I knew as my father said this that he'd betrayed me. My mother just laughed.

'Nancy, you don't give up, do you? You're a real obstinate Guernsey donkey. You take after my family, you really do.'

I refused to speak and held my silence all the way home. As we rode, my mother announced that Bruce and his father would definitely be joining us at Horseshoe Falls, though they wouldn't be staying on to camp the night.

'We'll have a lovely farewell picnic,' she said, unaware that I had been transfixing her with the darts of my rage and hurt every minute of the way back.

8

Bruce. Bruce Allotson, my age, my only remaining
English friend in Shillong now that most of the
English had left. I'd known him all my life. Bruce's
father was in the Forestry Commission in Assam;
he'd always been a close friend of my parents. So,
in the old days, was Bruce's mother, but she'd been
in England on leave when the war started and was
trapped there with Bruce's little brother. Bruce had
returned on an earlier ship with his father and so
during the war he'd spent a lot of time with us
because Mum felt so sorry for him. Ian Allotson was
on tour round the province all the time, so life was
difficult for them without Irene. Then at the end of
the war Irene had returned to India, but not to stay.
She'd met someone in England and wanted a
divorce. She had asked Bruce to go back with her
but he refused point blank to leave India. I was
convinced that he would understand my own feelings about leaving only too well.

When we arrived at the Horseshoe Falls, the Allotsons were already there. Bruce was standing on one
of the elephant rocks about to dive in. He waved
and disappeared in a neat arc with scarcely a splash.
I jumped out of the pony-trap and ran to the edge
of the pool as he swam into the shallows.

'Bruce, that was a perfect dive. Have you been
having lessons?'

'Hullo, Nancy. No, it's just my natural brilliance.'

He stood up; his wet ginger hair stuck to his head and his white freckled body looked inches taller since the last time I'd seen him. His shoulders had crept out and were almost as wide as his father's. He saw me staring and splashed me before falling back into the water. 'Go on, get into your swimming things and come in.'

'Did you get my letter?'

'Yes and I think you're dead lucky.' I was sure I hadn't heard right.

'My letter about being left in Guernsey—'

'Dead lucky.' He floated on his back. 'I can't wait to go back and start at a proper school in England.' He twisted his body over and swam away, shouting at me to hurry up as he did so.

Numbly I went back to help unload the pony-trap. My mother handed me bags and baskets and I carried them over to the tent which Abdul had already put up. 'Dead lucky.' Perhaps he was just trying to cheer me up about it. I dumped the stuff inside the hot tent which smelled musty and sweet and canvassy – a smell that I loved. Three camp-beds were already installed and a canvas cot for Clare. Abdul was tying the mosquito nets in place with neat fingers; Clare would be inside mine with me. The legs of the camp-beds were in little tin saucers of water, to stop ants crawling up. I could see the shadow of the hurricane lamp hanging outside, ready for the onset of darkness.

I waited for Abdul to finish and then started to change. For the first time in my life I was in no hurry to swim. I didn't really want to talk to Bruce if he was going to be like everyone else: unsympathetic.

34

'Nancy! Come on out! What on earth are you doing in there?' Bruce's fingers drummed on the outside of the tent. 'It's lovely in the water, really warm. Get a move on, I want to play water quoits.'

I ran after Bruce and as soon as I'd followed him into the delicious clear water I forgot how annoyed he'd made me. We played our quoits game for ages. We'd invented it years before; it involved jumping from rock to rock as we threw the ring. The rule was you couldn't throw the quoit more than once in a row from any rock. We fell in constantly and lost a point every time. We played it until we were weak from exertion and laughter. Then we went behind the waterfall, where you could stand looking through the whitish-green curtain of falling water from the narrow slimy rock ledge behind it. It was lovely to stick your arms out into the beating, rushing water and feel the force of it on your skin. The only problem you had to watch out for, apart from slipping, was the little black leeches that made for your bare body. It was easy to burn them off later with lighted cigarettes, but better not to get them in the first place.

We stood behind the noisy curtain of water and gasped at the power of it. It was majestic, mesmeric.

'How can you want to leave all this?' I shouted at Bruce.

'I didn't say I wanted to leave it.'

'Yes, you did. You said I was lucky and that you couldn't wait to go home.'

'You are lucky. This is the right time for you to change schools. I love India but I'm fed up with my school. All my best friends there have gone already. I can't go now until Dad leaves next year.'

35

'All I want is to stay until my father leaves too, Bruce.' Bruce didn't answer. He put his arms deeply into the water and then stood back again.

'I'm going to jump through.'

'Bruce, don't—'

'It's not that powerful. There isn't far to fall once I'm through it, and the pool's deep. I've always wanted to jump through a waterfall.'

With a wild triumphant yell, he was gone, blotted out instantaneously by the solid rush of water. Terrified of what I might find, I eased my way back along the ledge until I could climb free of the waterfall. My heart stopped. There was no sign of Bruce. His father was running and shouting something. Then I saw Bruce's head as he pulled himself, with difficulty, out of the main river which flowed strongly off to the right. His father was helping him ashore.

'What happened? Did you slip?' Bruce was grinning despite a few cuts and bruises.

'I jumped. It was easy.'

Ian Allotson exploded.

'That was a bloody stupid thing to do, bloody stupid. You might have knocked yourself out, and you'd have been swept away and certainly drowned. Don't you dare do that again.' Bruce's grin was a bit forced as he went off to change. 'Nancy, come here. Your back's covered with leeches.'

By the time they'd been burned off and plasters put on the punctures to stop the blood flowing into my clothes – leeches inject some chemical into your blood to stop it clotting – the fire was burning nicely. We'd all arrived mid-afternoon with a plan of

36

having a picnic supper together; as the shadows grew longer. Abdul started to cook and soon delicious smells overcame the ever-present scent of the surrounding pine-woods.

Bruce and I decided we'd go and find a good creeper to swing on; we searched for one we'd pulled free of its tree trunk the last time we'd been here which was spectacular. It swung right out over a deep gorge with another smaller waterfall crashing into it.

'Here it is. We'd better give it a good testing.' Bruce heaved violently at it, disturbing birds who flew off with a crisp flapping of startled wings. 'OK. I'll go first, that'll help to free it more.'

I pushed him and he sailed out over the gorge. A monkey leaped from tree to tree and disappeared so quickly I thought I'd imagined it until a second followed. Bruce's feet crashed through the undergrowth as he landed back near me.

'Great. Your go.' Out I went, the creeper creaking a bit but otherwise reassuringly solid. Leaves batted into my face as I went and I could hear the monkeys calling their strange 'hullock, hullock' to each other across the gorge. We had turn after turn.

We'd never needed to say much to each other, Bruce and I; all our lives we'd enjoyed doing the same things while knowing exactly how the other one felt. But today I couldn't help feeling for the first time that the silence between us wasn't easy any more; that Bruce wasn't quite with me. He looked at his watch a couple of times and was half-hearted about pushing the creeper. I knew it was a childish game, but I couldn't help being exhilarated by that creeper-swing; it was the best we'd ever found and I loved the feeling of the leaves on my face as I rose to the top of the arc. The golden light of the dropping sun caught the trees on the valley opposite; our side of the gorge was in shadow.

As soon as Bruce heard my father calling us he started off down the slope towards the picnic site. I stayed on the creeper a little while longer; 'hullock hullock' went the monkeys in the golden trees across the gorge. It was an aching, sad cry, an ancient cry that was nothing to do with man. I stayed on the creeper though it was now almost still and knew that my closeness to Bruce was over.

'Nancy! Nancy!' I saw my father searching through the trees for me.

'I'm coming.' He waited for me, a dark figure against the sunset. He put his arm around me.

'Enjoying yourself?'

'Yes.'

'You're angry with me for not taking your side over staying on, aren't you?'

'Yes.'

'Nancy, you know I'm a weak old fool when it comes to making decisions about you; all I want is for you to be happy and nearby if possible. But sometimes we have to ignore happiness and do things that are painful. I hate the thought of a divided family, I hate it. But Helen's right, you know; the time has come for you to leave this happy lotus-eating life and buckle down to a proper schooling.'

'I don't eat lotuses.'

'You know what I mean.'

'No, I really don't.'

'It was believed that if you ate lotus fruit you became dreamily vague and happy and lost all desire to return to your home.'

'Guernsey isn't home to me, that's the point. It may be home to Mum, but it's not to me. I've never been there. Why should I regard it as home?' I stopped on the path and turned to my father. 'And you don't like Guernsey much yourself, do you? I heard you say once to Bruce's father that, given the chance, you'd prefer to live in Devon.' There was a pause. My father sighed and squeezed my shoulder.

'Devon is where I was born. Naturally I'm attached to it. Guernsey is where Helen was born. She has a large number of relatives there and I have no-one left in Devon except a maiden aunt. Helen wants to return to her roots much more than I want to return to mine, so I've given in. It's the wisest decision for other reasons too. I'll pay much less tax in Guernsey and when I retire we're going to feel the pinch. We won't be well-off any more, Nancy; we'll have to watch every penny.' He started to walk on and I followed slightly behind him.

'So we'll be poor?'

'No, not poor, just not very well-off any more. This life will seem like a dream.' His shoulders slumped as we walked down towards the blazing camp-fire through the rapidly deepening darkness.

9

Hurricane lamps had been lit; they glowed in a ring round the rugs which had been laid out near the fire. The aroma of food made me realize I was famished. Abdul had prepared all my favourite things: spicy meat-balls, devilled chicken, onion bhaji, brinjal fritters. He'd made a stack of thin chapatis and what I liked doing was to fill one and roll it up. I put little meat-balls, brinjal fritters and a little rice on my first and made a lovely mess of myself eating it. Then I filled another with bits of chicken and some lettuce and our cook's lovely mango chutney and made slightly less mess but enjoyed it just as much. I passionately loved chapatis. I had them at almost every meal with things like butter and honey or marmite on them. I liked them much better than bread. Chapatis and peanut butter, chapatis and apricot jam. I could eat them forever. I preferred the simple dry chapati made of flour and water and cooked on a skillet to deep-fried, more elaborate versions like *puri* or poppadums, though I liked those too.

So I piled my extra large picnic chapatis with every good thing that was there and ate my way through that last meal at Horseshoe Falls. Bruce wasn't quite as keen on Indian food but he did pretty well; he just avoided the very hot dishes. We took our dessert – Indian ice-cream – on to the flattest elephant rock and sat surrounded by dark water. Dad put a hurricane lamp on the next rock to us and it made magical reflections.

'I wonder what the food's going to be like in Guernsey?' I wrapped my arms round my very full stomach. 'How can I manage without curries?'

'Do they eat French food in the Channel Islands?'

'I haven't a clue. What is French food?'

'I don't know. I've never been there. But I thought since France is so near . . .' He tailed off and we sat in silence. France, England, all Europe was unknown to me. It was unimaginably far away. I started to throw little crumbs of food into the water; immediately fish began to bite, causing shining ripples so that the water gleamed as if it was phosphorescent. The night air smelled of woodsmoke and pine-woods and river. I wanted the evening to go on for ever.

'My bum's cold,' said Bruce. 'Let's get back near the fire.'

'Alas, we must go,' said Ian Allotson after we'd played all sorts of games and laughed a lot. 'We must go. It's getting very late.'

Bruce jumped up and went off to their car. I thought for a moment he was going to get into it without saying goodbye, but instead he rootled inside it and came back with a package wrapped in bazaar paper. He shoved this at me, and said as I started to smile: 'It's only a bit of rubbish from the burra-bazaar.'

I opened it and found a little box with a hinged lid. It smelled sweetly of sandalwood and on the lid was carved an elephant with its trunk in the air.

'Thank you, Bruce.' If the grown-ups hadn't

been there I wouldn't have been so tongue-tied. 'The elephant's got a lovely expression.'

'It's nothing special.'

'I like it.'

'You can keep your jewellery in it,' said my mother. Why do parents have to make asinine remarks when there's no need to say anything? I ignored her.

'I've got nothing for you,' I muttered at Bruce when the others began to move towards the car. 'I feel dreadful.'

'It doesn't matter.'

'It does to me.'

'Send me something from Guernsey.'

'All right. I love my box.'

'I looked all through them to find the best elephant.'

And then we all stood awkwardly round the car as they prepared to leave. It was difficult to say goodbye; both Bruce and I knew that we probably would never meet again. Why should we? When his father retired they would be going to live in Scotland. But we promised to keep in touch and then in the end we all shook hands and that was it. I couldn't help feeling that this was a stupid way to take leave of my best friend but I couldn't do anything else. Indians would have been weeping and wailing and hugging each other. We just stood stiffly and said it all with our eyes.

10

I stood for some time in the tent when the car had gone, smelling the sandalwood box and feeling pierced with sadness. Perhaps it was going to be worse for Bruce than for me, because he was left behind in a place he now wanted to leave. The idea was disturbing. I put his present into my rucksack. I went back to the camp fire as I heard my mother say, 'Isn't it time that Nancy went to bed?'

'Not tonight. She can stay up as long as she likes on her last night at Horseshoe Falls. Let's play cards. Nancy, you choose the game.'

'Poker.'

'Poker it shall be.'

'I didn't bring any cards,' said my mother flatly. 'We don't usually play cards at picnics.'

'All is not lost.' My father fetched a box of dice from the car. 'We'll teach Nancy how to play Liar Dice instead.'

'Is that a good idea?'

'Of course it is. Now, Nancy, you only do well in this game if you're good at lying. Can I trust you to lie?'

We laughed and I turned out to be brilliant at lying and kept winning. It was nearly midnight when we finally stopped.

'We're both bankrupt, Nancy.' We'd been playing with tiny fir cones. 'Who'd have thought you'd be such an adept liar. You're a sly one.' My mother spoke laughingly, but gave me an uneasy look.

We piled up the fire and got ready for bed. Clare woke up and began to cry and it took some time to quieten her. I wondered whether her cries would attract large jungle beasts. I noticed Dad had his gun down beside the bed. We all lay inside our mosquito nets listening to the night sounds. Now that we were all silent, the jungle around us came alive. Against the ever-present rushing of the waterfall there were rustles and grunts and scratchings. Then suddenly the jackals started howling, one after another, an unearthly noise that had an echo of human child in it. They howled every night and we all said that if you turned your slipper over, they'd stop. It was strange how often they did.

'I haven't got my slippers,' I whispered.

'We'll just have to let them howl,' Mum whispered back. I could sense her smile.

But they stopped soon anyway and I fell asleep.

11

'I think you ought to have one of your tea-parties in the tree-house for Laughing and Rinjo.'

'But Mum, it's years since we did that.'

'Even so, it used to be very much part of your lives and I think it would be greatly appreciated. You can't leave them without some sort of farewell party.' I groaned.

'I'll only do it if we can have Indian sweetmeats.'

'You'll have sandwiches and cake and all that's part of an ordinary English tea. If you give them anything else they'll feel offended.'

So I went down to the godowns to invite them to tea next day. Laughing was squatting outside their door grinding something in a wooden bowl using a pestle made out of a piece of tree root, hard and shiny and worn from much use. She smiled and accepted but didn't seem inclined to chat. She was chewing betel.

'Where's Rinjo?'

'With the horses.' She nodded towards the stables and spat a pink shoot of juice as I left her.

Rinjo was giving Why Not *hart molesh*; he stood on an upturned bucket because he was so small and brought the leather pads hard down on her flanks. Thump, thump, THUMP. Why Not looked extremely contented and paid no attention to me.

'You're getting very good at that, Rinjo.' His muscles rippled in his thin arms as he worked. 'I came to ask you to tea tomorrow, tea in the tree-house like we used to have. But perhaps you'll be too busy.'

'I don't know . . .' But Purram Das had overheard me; he stopped working on Pempa and stuck his head round her.

'Of course you must go to Missy-baba Nancy's tea-party. You must wish her well in her new life in UK.' Pempa started to nip him because he'd stopped his attentions. *'Ari! Shaitan!'* he said as he always did and went back to work. Rinjo hadn't stopped; all he did was give me a shy smile.

'What time?'

'Four o'clock I suppose.' In the old days, the tea-parties had simply happened unplanned after an afternoon of playing together. 'I'll call you.'

'Very good.' He didn't add Missy-baba, but I had

the feeling he wanted to. He and Laughing had always called me Nancy; I did not want them to stop. I went back to the house feeling uneasy.

'I'm sure they were pleased, weren't they?' Mum said.

'They didn't seem it. I wish you hadn't made me ask them.'

'Nancy, for goodness' sake cheer up. Have them to tea in the house if you prefer, I don't care.' Mum was very ratty these days; she hated sorting and packing.

'No, the tree-house would be better.'

'Well, then. I can do without you making a mountain out of a molehill.'

Abdul brought a laden tray over to the tree-house next day with a disapproving expression on his face. He clearly thought the Memsahib's orders were well beyond what the ayah's children deserved to get. He left the tray at the bottom of the staircase and stalked off. On the tray were tomato sandwiches, egg sandwiches, chocolate biscuits and an iced cake. No chapatis and no sweetmeats. Ah well. I chased Fuss away and carried the plates up to the tree-house. I'd put a jamjar full of nasturtiums on the table. It all looked very pretty. I shut the door carefully in case Fuss got in and helped himself and went to call Laughing and Rinjo. They appeared at once out of their godown, both unaccustomedly smart, and the three of us climbed in silence into the tree-house.

'Some orange juice? Go on, help yourselves to food, whatever you like. Isn't Bahyong's new staircase good?' I started to chatter too much, but the silence was getting me down. 'Laughing, you're going back to your village soon, aren't you?'

'Yes. I leave when my mother goes with you to Bombay.' Congreeal and Abdul were accompanying us across India as far as the ship. 'Rinjo comes too.'

'Have another sandwich, Rinjo, don't wait to be offered. Are you looking forward to seeing all your relatives again?'

'I want to stay here and help with the horses until the Sahib and Mem are back, but my mother won't let me.'

'She doesn't trust Purram Das.' Laughing was smiling to herself.

'Why on earth doesn't she trust Purram Das?' Laughing gave a little titter and wiggled her shoulders.

'Shut your mouth.' Rinjo looked uneasy. Neither of them would say any more so eventually we changed the subject. Oh, how stiff that tea was. All our old easiness had gone; we might never have been friends at all. They were obviously longing to leave, so when the eating was over I asked them to help me carry the plates to the bottle-khana where the washing up was done. Then I told Rinjo to use the tree-house whenever he liked after I was gone; he nodded, but I wondered if he would. Anyway, Bahyong would probably stop him if he tried. Bahyong could be quite fierce when he felt like it.

When they'd gone I climbed back up into the tree-house feeling so depressed that I wanted to pour paraffin over the whole thing and set it on fire. What was the point of leaving it to be used by nobody; even Clare would never be old enough to play safely in it before she herself had to leave Assam for good. Then I heard claws on the wooden staircase and Fuss appeared in the doorway. I hugged him till he squeaked, I was so pleased to see him. I fed him what was left of the sandwiches and then the two of us sat on the top step and stared out over the jungle at the green hills all round and the faint blue smear in the distance that indicated the beginning of the Himalayan foothills. We were not high enough here to see those white peaks. Anyway the air wasn't clear enough; indeed, there were big rain clouds collecting. There was a distant grumble of thunder; Fuss growled. Then he suddenly went stiff and quivering, the way he behaves when there's an earthquake looming. He rushed off down the steps and hid himself away. Sure enough, minutes later the tree-house creaked and trembled. I was used to earthquakes; they were a common occurrence in Assam. Sometimes they were quite violent and the ground shook under us like jelly; this one today was the usual little quiver.

'Come down, Nancy!' Everyone had come out of our house as the earthquake went on and on, minute after minute. My mother came running towards me, stumbling a little because of the uncertain movement of the earth. 'It's safer on the ground.' I couldn't really see why, but I came down anyway.

The ground went on shaking and trembling for longer than usual, but the actual shock was very mild, as if there was someone under the earth's crust who couldn't help laughing gently. Or crying.

12

People, places, animals; it's awful having to say goodbye to all of them, but in a way I minded saying goodbye to the animals most. They couldn't understand, they had no knowledge of the future. Fuss was worried by all the packing, but often when we packed he had come along too, so he obviously held on to that. Every time the car door was open, he jumped in and objected if we tried to get him out.

Two days before we were due to leave, the suitcases and trunks came out of the loft above the garage. Fuss kept getting into them as soon as they were opened.

'He's going to be so upset when we go without him.'

'He'll be all right. He loves Gopal and Ram. But they'll have to keep him tied up for a while after we've gone, or he'll be off to Shillong looking for us. Dear old Fuss.' Mum picked him up out of a suitcase and kissed his nose and tried to cuddle him. But Fuss didn't want to be cuddled. He ran off down the garden and through the mimosa boundary and soon we heard him barking as he chased some alluring quarry. Then there was silence as the barks faded away. Mum and I got on with cleaning up the cases.

We never saw Fuss again. It was very strange; he just didn't come back. Not that evening, or the next day. We called and whistled and called until we were hoarse. Gopal and his son were so upset they went out with Dad searching for him without success. We never discovered whether he'd hunted something too big and fierce and been killed, or got stuck down a hole as Jack Russells often do, or been stolen by a passing hillman.

Fuss's disappearance made my parting with Why Not even more painful. I could hardly bear the thought that I'd definitely never see her again. Dad promised he wouldn't sell her just because I wasn't there to ride her and said that at the end he'd try and sell all three horses together because they'd been together so long. I had my final ride on the last day, not a long ride because the weather was bad, and Why Not snorted and blew through her nose and looked at me with her warm brown eyes. She tossed her head as she did when she was worried about anything. I'm sure she understood something unpleasant was happening to me, particularly when I was dragged back to the house crying.

We were leaving early the next morning, so by suppertime all the cases and trunks were already loaded on to the farm jeep, parked outside in the drive. Then Abdul served my last supper in the softly-lit dining-room, with its white plaster and black lathe walls and hanging paraffin lamp over the table that you could lower to fill and light. It had a handsome coloured shade and fat brass base with a curious design of dragons all round it. I stared at the lamp until my eyes smarted; I only realized now how much I enjoyed looking at it.

'You will bring that lamp when you come home, won't you?'

'We'll have electricity in Guernsey, we won't need it.'

'Promise you'll bring it anyway, I love it.'

'We could convert it, I suppose. Of course we'll bring it if it means so much to you. I love it too.' My mother looked dreamily round the room. 'Don't worry, Nancy, all the familiar things will come home. You'll have such a lovely time one day unpacking everything again and greeting old friends like the lamp.'

'Sometimes,' said my father, 'I think it would be better to leave most things behind and start afresh. We're all too attached to things, far too attached.'

I looked at the familiar red, blue and green place mats, at the old bone-handled knives and silver spoons and forks with Mum's initials on them. HOS, Helen Ozanne Sykes, born Queripel. A present from my grandparents, Abraham and Esmée Queripel. I looked at the familiar squat salt cellar and pepper pot and the deep blue glass mustard pot with its tiny silver spoon – I'd borrowed that once for Heather and got into trouble – and knew that it would comfort me to see them again. I looked at my father. He smiled.

'But don't worry, Nancy. I'm too attached myself. They'll come home.'

So both my parents kept telling me not to worry, but I wasn't feeling worried so much as extra perceptive of my surroundings that evening. I looked at the pictures on the walls – mostly water-colours of Indian birds and flowers done by a Chinese artist in Shillong. But there was a large picture of a beach in Guernsey over the fireplace, a rather clumsily-painted oil that my mother's sister Sophie had given her as a wedding present. *Rocquaine Bay with Fort Grey* was written on one corner.

'Aunt Sophie lives above that bay,' said my mother when she saw the direction of my glance. 'How exciting to think we'll be there in less than two months.'

Stiff white clouds like powder puffs, seagulls, stormy waves . . . I had never liked the picture much. And I had never in my life seen the sea.

Abdul served our pudding, which was Floating Island, my favourite. As we were finishing a knock came at the back door and we heard Abdul talking to Bahyong. Abdul sounded annoyed, Bahyong persistent.

'Sahib, the mistri wants to see the Missy-baba.' Abdul looked thoroughly disapproving. 'I told him you were all eating.'

'I've finished,' I said, spooning up the last island. 'Can't I go to see what he wants?' Without waiting, I got up and followed Abdul.

Bahyong was grinning all over his face and holding a parcel wrapped in the local Hindi newspaper.

'Missy-baba Nancy, I've come to say goodbye now because tomorrow I have to take my wife down to the Ganesh Das hospital.' He pushed the parcel at me. 'I made this for you, to remind you of your home and your friend Bahyong.'

I unwrapped the rough pinkish paper and there in my hands was a little model of my tree-house, doors, windows, thatch and all.

'Oh, Bahyong. It's beautiful. It's really beautiful.' I kissed him on his bristly cheek. He whistled

52

through his sparse teeth, his smile nearly splitting his face. He could see how thrilled and surprised I was. My parents had appeared behind me and I showed them the model.

'Goodness, Bahyong, when on earth did you do it?' My mother sounded even more surprised than me, because she usually knew exactly what was going on in the mistri-khana.

'I made it at home.'

'It's very well made, congratulations. What's the matter with your wife, by the way?'

'Stomach pains, sickness.' He didn't look very worried. 'So I must bid you all goodbye now. Sahib and Mem I will see again, but not you, Missy-baba.'

'Thank you for coming specially and thanks a million for my present. I'll keep it for ever.'

'See, the windows open.'

'It's perfect.'

Dad gave him his baksheesh and he salaamed and backed away with his hands together.

'Namaste.' Though I'd heard this phrase hundreds of times when Indians greeted each other or said farewell, it never sounded so poignant as it did that night. I too put my hands together.

'Namaste, Bahyong.'

'Namaste, namaste.'

13

Little feet pattered busily overhead while I lay in bed, unable to sleep. In the faint light I could see the imprints as their owners enjoyed themselves in our roof. Jackals howled. I thought of poor Fuss, whom we'd called again before going to bed, hoping that his mischievous face would come guiltily out of the darkness after two days good hunting. I thought of all the people I'd said goodbye to in the last week: my schoolfriends; the workers down on the farm; the shopkeepers I knew in the town, specially Morello's, the Italian confectioner whose chocolate Easter eggs had been such a high point each year. Having made the shells out of good quality chocolate, he'd fill them with his own fondants and sweets and decorate the outsides with wonderful curls and twirls and your name in white icing. Morello's made me think of Firpo's chocolates, which arrived from Calcutta in large flat shiny red square tins, with Firpo's written in gold in the middle. The smell and taste of those chocolates nestling in their corrugated brown paper cups was even better than Morello's chocolate eggs. Italians making chocolate in India . . .

I was just wondering what Italy was like when I noticed that the scrabbling footprints on the ceiling were shadowed in pinkish grey instead of just murky grey. My bedroom led off the playroom, which was next to the dining-room. My parents' bedroom also led off the playroom on the other side and Clare now slept in the playroom. Our doors were all half-glassed and the glass was covered with thin silk gathered at the top and bottom on rods. I peered round my door and froze with horror. Not only was the playroom full of brighter pink light, but it was too warm. And the heat and light came from the door into the dining-room. The dining-room was on fire.

Clare was peacefully asleep in her cot. I tore the mosquito net aside and grabbed her before running into my parents' room.

'Mum! Dad! Quick, quick, the house is on fire!'

After that everything moved so fast that it's a blur of frantic activity in my memory. My parents shouted for water, the servants woke up and hurried towards the house doing up their clothes, eyes dazed with horror. Everyone started to pull things out of the house. The thatch above the dining-room was growing little shoots of red, tongues which became larger by the second. Abdul rushed past shouting excitedly that he was off to the main farm to telephone for the fire engine. He jumped on his bike and tore off into the darkness.

I saw my mother carrying, single-handed, a chest of drawers down the veranda steps, a chest she could normally not even have lifted. I went to fetch more from the bedroom, but she stopped me.

'Keep away from the house! Your job is to look after Clare.' She rushed into the bedroom again. My father was the other side of the house, rescuing what he could from the sitting-room and yelling directions at servants.

We'd put Clare, still asleep, into the front of the jeep. I went over to see if she was all right and found her standing against the steering wheel bawling her head off, her hair on end and her eyes full of fear. I got in with her and held her tight until she stopped crying, then we both sat and watched our beloved home burn to the ground. There was nothing to be done; we hadn't got enough water to make any difference and the fire engine arrived after a five-mile drive on twisting roads long after the roof had fallen in. Villagers from all round had crept up the drive and were standing watching the spectacle of the burra-sahib's house reduced to cinders. Then the dawn came, pink and fresh, a very different pink from the horrible light that had roused me. The blackened remains of walls smouldered in the growing light; there was an acrid smell in the air. Slowly the villagers and servants went back to their homes, to perform their washing ceremonies and say their prayers for a safe future.

The useless fire engine went back to Shillong and for a while the Sykes family were alone beside the ruin of their house. Mum and Dad were still in pyjamas, blackened and filthy now. Underneath the dirt their faces were grey. Clare, thank goodness, had gone back to sleep in the jeep. I stood and looked at all our poor possessions, all higgledy-piggledy on the lawns and paths. Except for the things in the dining-room and playroom, most of our stuff had been saved. And there in the jeep were the cases full of clothes, the trunk with all my things in it, the box of Clare's toys for the journey.

Mum, Dad and I stood for long minutes with our arms around each other. At last Dad said: 'I could have happened two nights ago, before we'd packed. We're lucky.'

Mum started to cry, great shaking sobs.

'How are we going to leave this place in a few hours time to go and catch a train? But if we don't we'll miss that ship. Oh Bernard, what are we going to do?'

'We're just going to go. I've been thinking about it. Mohan is the most efficient farm manager I've ever had. He's bound to be up here soon and I'm going to leave the rebuilding for him to organize for the moment. We'll store all our stuff in the big garage; it's got a good lock on it and all our servants will be here to keep an eye on things.'

Mum continued to cry for a bit, and then she said, trying to laugh through her tears:

'I never thought I'd see meat roasting inside the fridge.'

At that moment John came out of the bobaji-khana with a tray loaded with breakfast; since his cookhouse was twenty feet from the back door, it had escaped untouched. Abdul had found a camping table and put an assortment of chairs round it. Clare was woken up and the four of us had what we usually have for breakfast, but in a setting that was surreal. The acrid smell was still strong, beams were still slowly burning.

Then Mohan arrived full of horrified sympathy, followed by other friends from Shillong who'd heard of our tragedy. We were offered baths, help, loving care. Within two hours I had stroked Why Not's nose for the last time and said a tearful goodbye to Purram Das, Guru, Gopal and Ram, John, Happy, Laughing and Rinjo. Then, Dad and I led the way in the jeep, followed by Mum, with Congreeal and Abdul and Clare. I looked back and saw the ragged row of servants standing in front of the blackened stumps that had been our house and wept all the way to Shillong.

14

We set off a day late, which Dad said would still not make us miss the ship because he'd allowed an extra day in Calcutta to say goodbye to our friends there. In fact, we had all collapsed from exhaustion and delayed shock when we got to a friend's house in Shillong. Dad and Mum had so many decisions and arrangements to make as a result of the fire that they needed all the afternoon and evening. I slept most of the day; I didn't want to, but I couldn't keep awake. And I was ready for sleep again at bedtime that night; a heavy weight seemed to be pressing down on my brain.

We all felt better the following morning and as we set off for the sixty mile drive to the nearest station at Amingaon, I could feel the first stirrings of excitement creeping past my distress at leaving Shillong behind. The drive down to the plains was always one I loved.

Amingaon is on the other side of the great Brahmaputra River and so we had to descend four thousand feet to Pandhu Ghat, where we would catch the ferry across the river. In the first ten miles from Shillong we had to wind our way down two thousand feet; the road was an endless hairpin bend. The whole road was only wide enough for one car, so the Motor Company had a one way system: you went down in their cars to a half-way point called Nongpo, then you transferred to the cars which had just come up and now turned to go back. The cars you'd started in turned too and went back to Shillong. At stages along the road there were gates to control the traffic; Nongpo was the third gate, where there was a rest house which served tea and light refreshments. My ears had been popping as we descended, so I was glad to drink orange juice and walk about. We always met people we knew at Nongpo.

'What on earth are you all doing here today?' said a familiar voice. 'I thought you were catching yesterday's train.' It was Ian Allotson, without Bruce.

'We were delayed by a disaster.' Ian was appalled to hear about our fire and promised to go up to the farm every week to check that all was well with our possessions. Then we were summoned to the cars and he went on up while we continued down.

'Lucky meeting,' said Dad. 'I trust Ian above everyone.'

Burnihat Gate, Thanapara Gate and then the plain straight road to Pandu Ghat. As we got out of the cars dozens of shouting Indians descended on us, keen to carry our luggage to the *ghat* or quay. There was so much noise and confusion Clare started to yell and I didn't blame her. I hung on to Dad's hand and my bag in which I'd managed to fit the model of the tree-house on top of my two books, sponge-bag, hair-brush and pyjamas for use during the long train journey.

The ferry, a newly-painted white paddle-steamer, was waiting. It was on its way up the Brahmaputra to Fezpur and Dibrugarh and beyond; we would only be on it for the hour it took to cross the mile-wide river. The water was creamy brown and full of boats, country boats with patched home-made sails and large rudders and long thin fishing boats which lay close to the water in the middle and curled up gracefully into points at each end. There were other ferries; a big one passed going down-stream towards the Ganges, the Sundarbans and Calcutta.

'It's a pity we couldn't go down to Calcutta by ferry,' I said to Dad who'd just come to stand beside me at the rails.

'I know. It would have taken too long, alas.'

'I'll never forget that trip.'

When I was six my parents had made the return trip from Calcutta to Assam by ferry. It was the most exciting journey I'd ever had; the trip took two weeks and I remembered every detail as if it had been yesterday. I'd had a little white cabin next to my parents. The bathroom with its shiny tin tub and wooden thunderbox was much smarter than ours at the farm. I'd made my first good friend on that trip – she was the eight-year-old daughter of tea-planters travelling back to their Assamese planta-tion. Lucy and I stood for hours on the foredeck by the flagstaff and watched the river. We saw por-poises by the hundred, we saw monkeys in the watery jungles of the delta called the Sundarbans and huge man-eating crocodiles called muggers. We shivered when our ayahs told us that the muggers' stomachs were full of bangles, children's bangles. There are tigers in the Sundarbans, but we never saw one though we watched until our eyes went dry with the effort.

Then the strange leafy green world of the

Sundarbans had ended and the steamer chugged on up the open Ganges and then turned into its great tributary, 'our' river, the Brahmaputra. Not that it looked any different from the Ganges; they were both immense creamy brown stretches, almost colourless in the distance. Sometimes the banks were so distant you could only see a thin darker line. At other times we went close to the banks; Lucy and I would gaze at thatch-roofed villages, at the women and children in the river who would wave and shout as they stood thigh deep in the water. But mostly the shore would be too far away to see people as more than sticks.

I was deliriously happy all during that trip. I loved Lucy – I'd have been upset to know then that I'd never see her again. She and I liked watching the Muslim crew at prayers; at sunset they would stop whatever they were doing and all kneel down on the lower deck in neat rows. Silent ourselves, we would hang over the rail above. Their bent, concentrated bodies somehow awed us.

'How do they know which way Mecca is?' I whispered.

'It's to the west.'

'But the boat keeps turning as it follows the river.'

'I expect their prayers go up just the same.' Lucy said this so firmly that I could almost see the prayers floating up through the birds which always flew with the steamer.

'I'll never forget it,' I repeated.

'Nor will I,' said Dad. 'Do you remember the

huge muggers? Much bigger than any I've seen around here.'

'I hate muggers.' My father laughed. I knew why he laughed. There's a story about me my parents are always telling, how when I was about Clare's age I was photographed on a dead mugger Dad had shot, happily sitting on its great scaly head, smiling under my topi. What the photo doesn't show is that immediately afterwards the mugger started to move and Mum had to snatch me to safety while my father got his gun and finished it off properly. I don't remember a thing about it, but there's a photo of me sitting on a mugger to prove it happened.

At that moment the steamer was cast off and the paddles started to churn up the water. Someone fell into the water off the ghat and the crowd cheered and laughed as he came up grinning and swam ashore. Then the south bank receded fast and in no time Pandu was just a blur on the horizon surrounded by palm-trees. Way behind it was the dusty blue shape of the Khasi Hills, with the bump of the Shillong Peak higher than anything else. I thought of my rides on it and the Horseshoe Falls and the Crinoline Falls and the Elephant Falls and the Elysium Falls pouring down endlessly whether I was there or not and I felt as if my heart was being pulled out of me and left on the Assam shore.

THE JOURNEY

'But we are having a reservation for you yesterday, My Sykes. Today First Class is full. Also Second.' The station-master looked hot and cross.

'I sent a message that we were unavoidably delayed.'

'I am receiving no message.' Dad started to get annoyed. Mum sat down on our luggage and put her head in her hands. I stood beside her, leaden; back into my mind came those fierce flames consuming our house like a monster and leaving a gap, a vacuum behind; I could picture our garden but the focus of my image no longer existed. The hubbub all round me continued, but I was lost in mourning our house.

'Right everyone, we're going to have a goods van to ourselves. Come on Helen, cheer up. It's going to be fun.'

'You mean, it will have to be fun.' Mum looked exhausted as she collected us together. Followed by the coolies with our luggage, we trailed off down to a goods van at the rear, watched by the entire train. Tea-planters and their families looked out of the First Class windows, smug and secure in their seats.

Dad insisted the van was tidied and organized

for us: he got the station-master to make sure that the bulky goods were out of the way at one end and the rest of the trunks and bales were put so that they made platforms for us to sit on and sleep on. Blankets were brought and little square railway pillows, and finally the station-master himself brought a zinc tub full of ice and put it in the middle of the floor – all compartments were cooled in this way.

'There sir, now you are goods van First Class,' he said and chuckled at his joke for ages.

At last the little train pulled out and we started the long journey towards Calcutta. This train, part of the Assam-Bengal Railway, would take us as far as Parbatipur Junction, where we would transfer on to the big train for Calcutta. The little train was very noisy and rocked and bumped continually, but we were surprisingly comfortable on our bales and trunks because there was plenty of room to lie down and stretch out. Hurricane lamps were lit, even though Dad managed to prop open a sliding door to give us extra air and light; Abdul and Congreeal sat at one end of the van and in no time Abdul had brewed up some tea, and warmed the soup and even made chapatis. It turned out to be much more fun than being in an ordinary compartment. We sang silly songs like 'Ten Green Bottles' and played games and even Clare was so happy that she went to sleep like a lamb in a makeshift cot between two bales covered with gunny. We were only able to go to the lavatory when the train stopped at a station, but the Assam-Bengal line was so small and friendly that they always waited for the last person to get back on the train.

The train often stopped for no apparent reason: perhaps wild animals on the line, or perhaps the driver just felt like it. The silent darkness outside smelled of jungle and rotting vegetation and the cries of animals and night-birds were all round us, uncomfortably close. Dad and I gazed out through our gap, across the bottom of which was a trunk for safety. In the dark shadows of trees and bushes we saw eyes gleaming as the beings in the wild watched this strange, long, noisy thing, full of lights.

I was so sleepy by the time we changed trains that I let the crash and clatter of the junction wash over me and fell asleep the moment I lay down on my bunk in our new compartment – Dad's re-arrangements did not misfire this time. When I woke the big train was stationary. I saw Dad standing out in the corridor and joined him.

We stood looking out at the early morning mist, at the sun touching the palm-trees in a clump nearby; we heard crows cawing, and smelled the dew-soaked earth, the dung on the fields, the wood-smoke of village fires that were invisible but not far away because the acrid smell was fresh. Only Dad and I were awake; we stood there in silence and when the train started up again Dad put his arm round me.

'The smells of India are what everyone misses,' he said.

As the train moved smoothly through the flat landscape, the morning mist started to thin. The cattle standing in the fields near each village lost their ghostly look as the sun rose free of the horizon, still a red disk without power. I saw motionless holy men; one sitting on top of a tree stump, his arm stuck permanently above his head as if he was trying to catch God's attention. People had put offerings round the base of his tree stump: flowers, food.

'Their muscles atrophy,' said Dad. 'That arm is useless now.'

A cow was eating the holy man's offerings and no-one did anything about it, cows being sacred. I've always thought it was a funny animal to choose; it would have been better to choose horses. Or elephants.

From Calcutta to Bombay we were on a brand new train, with air-conditioning. It smelled of fresh rubber flooring and new plush seating. But the windows were sealed and so we could never open them in the morning and get the fresh new day into our nostrils. I began to hate the air-conditioning; I felt trapped by it and cheated. So when the train stopped at a station I had to get out, just to smell the ordinary smells of India again.

By the time the three day journey from Calcutta to Bombay was over we'd all had enough of trains. We'd been in them on and off for five days and we were all filthy and sticky, despite the air-conditioning and the little basin with hot and cold water in the corner of our compartment. My hair, which was thick, curly and long, was in such a tangled state I never wanted anyone to come near it again with a brush and comb. I'd given up early in the journey and now all I wanted was for it all to be cut off. Bombay was much hotter than Assam;

my hair felt like a dark brown carpet on my head, a horrid matted carpet.

When we got to our hotel I noticed it had a hairdressers on the ground floor. 'Ladies and Gentlemans Select Coiffure.' After breaking my comb on the outer layer of tangles, I decided that if I did nothing else in Bombay, I would have my hair cut short. My mother had vetoed it up to now; she liked my long hair.

'No, Nancy, not here for heaven's sake. At least wait until you're settled in Guernsey.'

'I can't stand it a minute longer. I can't get a comb through it anyway.'

'Come here.' Very irritably Mum tried to pull her comb through my hair and broke it too. 'This is ridiculous. Why didn't you get Congreeal to comb it on the journey instead of letting it get like this.'

'You did say I had to get used to doing things for myself.'

Mum threw her comb away and suddenly gave in. I was left in the hands of Madame Rosina of 'Select Coiffure', while everyone else went for a walk on the sea-front, two streets away. I had refused even to go to see the sea for the first time until I'd had my hair cut; it wasn't vanity, it was a feeling that I needed to be as different as possible before I saw such an important part of the earth's surface for the first time.

Madame Rosina hacked away at the matted brown curls with an expression of distaste. Then she washed what was left and trimmed my hair so that it curled short all over my head in what she called a 'bubble cut'. I couldn't believe how different I looked. Best of all I was pounds lighter. I floated out of the main door of the hotel into the crowded street, dying to show my parents. I decided to try and find the sea-front myself and imagined their surprise as they saw a taller, more grown-up looking Nancy with ears that no longer stuck out because her hairstyle covered them.

I didn't find my parents but I did see the sea. I stared at the pounding greyish-blue breakers of the Arabian Sea and was surprised at the number of waves and their frequency. I'd somehow imagined the sea would be less insistent. I loved the salty smell and the feel of the wind in my short hair. Then I looked over at the great towers at the far edge of the sea and knew they were the Parsi Towers of Silence, where according to their religion the Parsis lay their dead to be picked clean by vultures and the weather. I saw the ever-circling vultures against the blue sky and found them sinister. Then I looked at the Arabian Sea again and couldn't help feeling a shudder of excitement that tomorrow I would be on it, sailing off west.

Saying goodbye to Congreeal and Abdul was dreadful. They were so much part of my life that I couldn't believe I really would never see them again. They insisted on coming to the docks to see us off and there they stood, a few feet apart, not talking to each other, as we boarded the ship and then went to the side so that we could wave goodbye. It seemed very important that we stood there until they were out of sight. I waved and waved. I knew poor Congreeal was going to hate the journey back to Shillong with only Abdul to cheer her up. He was used to travelling, she wasn't. Dad had given them enough money to travel the whole way Second Class but he knew they wouldn't. They'd join the thick crowds in Third and pocket the difference.

My mother kept saying that our ship, the *City of Exeter*, was an old heap but I didn't think it was too bad. It had been used as a troop ship during the war and had not been refurbished because this was its last journey before the scrap-yard. The engines made a lot of noise and the paintwork was streaked with rust.

My mother was upset because we were separated from Dad: all the men had to sleep in the lower decks in sort-of dormitories, while the women and children shared the cabins. Mum, Clare and I had to share our cabin with two women, a Mrs Railton and her daughter Julie. They slept on the porthole side and we three shared the other two berths.

'I hope your baby is quiet,' was the first thing Mrs Railton said to us. Mum just smiled since Clare certainly wasn't quiet, as they would soon find out for themselves. The Railtons did not smile back; they hardly ever smiled, they did everything with pursed-up mouths and frowns. The daughter, Julie, looked as old as the mother to me; they could have been sisters, except that Mrs Railton had a moustache and Julie's hadn't grown yet. They wore beige clothes and curious underwear. I used to lie on my top berth reading and sometimes flick a glance at them as they collected their clothes before going off to the bathroom to change and wash in private. There was a basin in the cabin but they never used it.

'Your daughter's very nosy,' said Mrs Railton on the second day. 'Please ask her to have a little thought for others. It's bad enough being on this overcrowded ship without being stared at all the time by rude children.' And she walked off in a huff.

I hated the Railtons from then on. Mum had started to give Clare a bath in the basin and I could see she was very upset. She knew I hadn't been particularly nosy and she said nothing to me about it. We had to endure the Railtons for six weeks and that was that. But it was going to be grim.

Aden, the Suez Canal, the Mediterranean, Gibraltar, the Bay of Biscay . . . our route was full of names I'd heard all my life and which evoked vivid pictures in my mind. The reality was sometimes disappointing. I'd imagined Aden as a desert full of fierce Arabs on camels, and it didn't seem that different from a port like Bombay except that it was surrounded by scorched cliffs of sandy rock. The hubbub in the harbour was the same as in India. Mum and Dad went ashore briefly and brought back Turkish Delight, which I'd never tasted before and found delicious.

Even more disappointing than Aden were the Bitter Lakes; I'd expected the ship to sail through waters that looked or smelled different. And the Red Sea was as blue as the Bitter Lakes. I think it was then that I decided I had to wipe my imagination clean and forget all my preconceived ideas.

Then the Suez Canal stopped being disappointing and became fascinating. We glided slowly between the two banks; speed was kept low to avoid a bow wave which would erode the sand on each side. Sad-looking rusty ships, casualties of the war, lay at odd angles, empty; loose bits of superstructure clanged and clattered in the hot wind. Often we saw camels lifting their heads and staring at us with their snooty expressions.

Port Said was wonderful; lots of Egyptians came on board, including the famous gullee-gullee men who did amazing conjuring tricks with little fluffy chicks. One gullee-gullee man pretended to find a chick behind Mrs Railton's ear. Since she had rather fierce eyes like a hen's and yellow-grey permed curls, the sight of the little chick going 'peep, peep, peep' from behind her ear made everyone laugh. Mrs Railton went very red and moved well away from the gullee-gullee man. Then Mum got her handbag open to put some money in the hat going round and there to her immense surprise she found another little chick! I could have watched those conjurors all day, but soon they were shepherded off the ship and instead we watched the boys in the water diving for coins thrown from the deck. They literally swam like eels, snaking down as gleaming coins sank through the water. We all went ashore in the afternoon and Mum and Dad took us to a shop called Simon Artz – at least that's what it sounded like – full of marvellous leather goods which smelled even better than the leather shops in the burra-bazaar at Shillong. They bought me my first wallet, dark red leather with a neat brass clasp and a matching purse for coins. They bought leather slippers for our grandparents and Aunt Sophie in Guernsey and a purse rather like mine for each of Aunt Sophie's children, my first cousins. The sight of four purses on the counter made me realize, as nothing else had, how different my life was going to be. I'd be sharing a house with Agnes, Basil, the twins Marie and Pierre . . . all older than me, but not much. I felt sick with apprehension and was glad when we got back into our gharry and started to drive back to the docks. Sitting in an open gharry going at a slow trot is much the best way of seeing a new city. I forgot again about Agnes, Basil, Marie and Pierre.

As we drew away from the coastline of Egypt and it faded out of sight, lots of English people who were going home for good rushed to the rail and threw their topis into the sea.

'Goodbye, the East! Next stop Europe!' shouted one man.

The topis bobbed in the wake of the ship, some brim up and some brim down, all looking like a strange type of turtle riding the waves. I noticed Mrs Railton and Julie coming up late to the rail with their hats and throwing them over with their little pursed mouths actually smiling.

'Good riddance!' said Julie.

Topis are made from cork covered with fabric, so they would float for miles. I could imagine heaps of them on an Egyptian beach looking from a distance like weird brown jellyfish, or perhaps turtles again.

My topi was packed in my trunk in the hold and I intended to keep it ready for that day when I went back to India.

A bad storm hit us in the Mediterranean; it blew up during the night and a sudden big wave poured through our open porthole and gave us all a dreadful fright. I saw my new slippers – more nice leather from Simon Artz – floating about when I peered over the edge of my berth. There was a good inch of water on the floor. The Railtons started to whimper. Mum leaped to the porthole to shut it before another wave came in and then tried to mop up the sea-water with towels while the ship bucked and wallowed.

Then Clare woke and began to scream. She didn't want me, so Mum had to stop mopping and get back into the berth to comfort Clare. The Railtons moaned uselessly. The storm raged all night; at one point all the lights went out. It was terrifying. When they came back on again, there was a knock on our door and there stood my father, swaying about in his dressing gown and looking very cheerful.

'Surviving, all of you?'

'Just about.' Mum looked rather white.

'The poor old ship's getting quite a bashing. Let's hope the Bay of Biscay isn't any worse than this.' Dad picked up one of my wet slippers. 'Not very wise to leave a porthole open.'

'We were all asleep when the storm hit us.'

'Mr Sykes, does anyone know how long this storm is going to last?' quavered Mrs Railton. The ship rolled wildly.

'Oops.' My father staggered backwards laughing. 'Not much longer I should guess. These Mediterranean storms are violent but short. I'm just going to put my nose out on deck to see what size the waves are.'

'Can I come?' I was already out of the berth but

my mother told me sharply to stay put. Dad winked at me and shut the cabin door as the ship rolled wildly again. He was humming 'A life on the Ocean Wave'.

'Your husband's very jolly,' said Mrs Railton, her mouth a thin line. Julie moaned. The lights went off again.

In the morning the sea was calm and blue, the wind light. The seagulls were on duty all round the ship as usual, as if the storm had never happened. A school of dolphins kept pace with us for a while and then suddenly were gone. The ship stopped only to refuel at Gibraltar, so no-one was allowed ashore. I stared at my first bit of Europe and found it strange that for the first time in my life all I could see ashore were light-coloured skins.

We left the blue skies behind us as we rounded Cape St Vincent into the Atlantic. From then on there was grey land – if it was visible at all – cold winds and then rain when we got past the northern tip of Spain and began our crossing of the Bay of Biscay. It wasn't rain like monsoon rain, pouring straight down, warm endless sheets of rain. I'd liked being out in that rain; once you were soaked, it felt lovely on your skin. This Atlantic rain was like needles, blown into you by the cruel wind. I didn't have enough warm clothes; my thick things were down in the hold.

'Is it going to be cold like this in Guernsey?'

Mum and I were in one of the lounges, with Clare asleep on a seat beside us. Mum was sewing a button back on to a shirt with impatient jabs. She hadn't done any sewing for years; Ahmed did it all, even the mending.

'Only in the winter,' she said defensively. 'The summers can be lovely.'

'But isn't it still summer now? It's only just September.'

'We've been unlucky with the weather. This bad patch will pass. You'll have to get used to the weather being changeable, Nancy. It's not like India, day after day the same.' She sighed and bit off the thread. 'Come on, let's go for a quick blow round the deck. Clare is out for a good while.'

We battled against the stiff cold wind until we reached the stern of the ship where there was some shelter. We gazed out over the gunmetal-coloured waves.

'Imagine, Nancy, soon we'll be sailing past little Guernsey, as we go up the English Channel. We won't be close enough to see it, of course. But it's a pity the *City of Exeter* can't just drop us off. Take a detour.' As Mum looked out over the grey sea she had tears in her eyes, either from the wind or her feelings.

'I'm cold,' I said. 'Let's go back inside.' I wished I could feel excited about arriving in Guernsey. As we got closer I was beginning to feel cold inside as well as out. In my summer dress and cardigan and light coat and cotton socks I was cold, cold, cold. And my mind pictured all those unknown relatives, grandparents and aunts and uncles and cousins, and then I was apprehensive as well as cold.

Clare was grizzling; Mum put her harness back on and off they went round the deck again. When they got back Clare was wailing about something.

Mum wasn't used to looking after Clare every minute of the day and it made her short-tempered.

'I wish we had Congreeal with us,' I said.

Mum didn't answer; she just picked Clare up and headed for our cabin. Clare's wails were now screams of anger. I decided I'd go and find my father; at this time of day he was usually reading in a deckchair near the bar, with a whisky and soda beside him. He was exactly where I thought he would be.

'Hullo, my old Nance. You look very glum. What about a ginger beer to cheer you up?'

'Yes, please.'

'Where's Helen?'

'Clare's in a paddy. They've gone to the cabin. Let's hope the dear Railtons aren't down there too.'

'Poor Helen. This boat trip hasn't been much fun for her.'

I'd noticed that my father wasn't much help with Clare. He tended to melt away when she was being difficult. It hadn't been obvious in India, but it was now. He fetched me my glass of ginger beer. I sat beside him and looked out at the waves on the port side; they were the same choppy grey waves as the other side, but they went on and on with no land until you got to North America. I didn't much like the sound of the word North. I'd been coming up the Northern Hemisphere and it had been growing colder all the time. North . . . North America, North Sea, North Pole. They all had a freezing ring to them. South and East and West were nicer, softer words than North. You opened your mouth more to say them, they had esses and gentler vowels.

'Dad, if I really hate being in Guernsey, *really*

hate it, will I have to stay on by myself?' My father sipped his whisky before he answered.

'That's not a fair question, Nancy. If I say yes, you'll think us horrid and cruel, and if I say no, you'll make sure you really hate it just to come back to India with us.' He tapped my glass. 'True or not true?'

'Well . . .'

'And I don't think you're going to hate Guernsey. Why should you? It's a lovely little island, full of beautiful beaches and for the first time you'll be able to make lots of friends of your own age and see them whenever you want to because they're not miles and miles away on a tea-plantation or whatever. You're going to enjoy that much more than you realize. You've been too much alone.'

'Mum keeps saying I'm very young for my age.'

'I know and I wish she wouldn't. I don't think you are. In some ways I think you're old for your age.' I stared at my father, a slow delight filling me. 'Your attitude to India is quite mature, for instance. Most children don't love scenery and nature for themselves, but you do. You seem to love India for the same reasons an adult would, for the reasons I do.'

'So you can understand why I want to go back.'

'Of course I can. Of course I can. But consider this. You may grow to love the scenery in Guernsey and find the same delight in your surroundings there one day.'

I didn't find this at all possible, but I said nothing. At that moment Mrs Railton and Julie walked past with their bags of knitting. They'd been

77

sitting wrapped in rugs on the windy side of the ship.

'I told you we should have moved,' we overheard Julie say. 'It's ever so much warmer this side.'

'Too late now,' said Mrs Railton sharply. 'It'll be dinner in half an hour, we ought to go and change.' They ignored us completely.

'Hope they enjoy Clare,' I murmured.

'It will be lovely to get off this ship,' said Dad when they were out of earshot. 'It's been very hard for the three of you to share with those two dragons. I've been all right . . . travelling steerage is not what I'd choose but it really hasn't been too bad considering. Poor old *City of Exeter*. She wasn't built for such a crowd of us.'

'When are we due to dock at Southampton?' Because of engine trouble we were running nearly a week late. The ship was audibly limping along, as if she was glad it was her last voyage. I'd grown very fond of her, of her decks and gangways and thick encrusted white paint; the smells of oil and rust and rope mingling with the salt air.

'Tomorrow, late morning if all goes well. Then a few days in London and on down to Weymouth to catch the Channel Islands mail-boat.' I knew all this but I didn't mind my father telling me it all again. When you've been on a ship for six weeks you run out of things to talk about. 'I must go and change for dinner myself and you'd better go and see if Helen could do with a hand.'

Children's tea was at five-thirty so I'd already eaten; though I could have had dinner with the adults it was decided that I shouldn't, so that I could keep an eye on Clare while my parents had their dinner in peace and quiet. The main sitting for dinner was at seven and it left me with the worst period of my day. I had to stay in the cabin in case Clare woke up and got frightened on her own. It was utterly boring. I'd read all my books a hundred times by then and all the books in the ship's library that interested me. There was nothing for me to do except play patience.

'Shsh. She's just dropped off,' whispered Mum. 'The Railtons were quick this evening and they didn't keep her awake for once.' Clare loved to watch them getting themselves ready for dinner and as she was so little they couldn't really complain.

Mum stood there in her satin petticoat made for her by Ahmed. She'd given him some old lace to set into it and the result was in my opinion a lot prettier than many of the dresses that went on top. Mum pulled on her best dress, green crêpe with long sleeves and a sweetheart neckline. It was called that because the neckline was heartshaped, but I didn't like it, neither the name nor the neckline. Mum nearly always wore green, or sometimes cream or rust or brown.

'Why don't you wear red? Or yellow?'

'Green's my colour.' Her bright green eyes met mine in the mirror over the wash basin. She was brushing her long brown hair before she put it up on top of her head.

'You'd look nice in red.'

'I'd feel like a pillar-box. You wait and see how fat and round and red they are, waiting for your letters at the corners of the streets.' She put a pair of dress clips in the corners of her neckline and powdered her face. She was cheering up by the minute; the long day of looking after Clare was in its best phase.

'Green suits you because of your eyes, I suppose,' I said. I felt doubtful; I thought this green dress made her look a bit sallow, actually. 'I look awful in green but then that's because I've got blue eyes.'

'Well, you look good in blue and I simply can't wear it.' She dabbed a little lipstick on and then blotted most of it off. She was very tentative about make-up, my mother. She put a dab of scent behind her ears and then some behind mine. It was Coty's *L'Aimant*, very sweet-smelling. Dad had bought it for her in Bombay, because she'd lost her last bottle in the fire.

'It was lucky we didn't lose our clothes,' she said for the umpteenth time. She'd obviously thought of the fire again for the same reason I had. 'So lucky.' She put more scent on, this time on her wrists. 'I still live through the whole thing every day, I can't help it.'

'I had a dream about it last night. We were having a picnic on a grassy patch, all smooth, where our house had once been.'

'Don't let's talk about it now.' She twirled round. 'Is my petticoat showing?'

'No. Are you going to the dance tonight?'

'We'll go for a bit, but I'll come back before it starts so that you can go and watch your father in the tug-of-war.'

'You ought to wear red, you know. I'm sure it would suit you.'

'I'd feel wrong in it.' She dug out her good suede shoes, also green.

80

'By the way, what colour's the uniform at the College?' Mum paused before answering.

'It used to be bottle green. It could have changed, of course. See you at about half-past eight, darling.'

Bottle green. *Bottle green.* Mum went out of the cabin and I sat in misery on my berth. Of all the colours in existence, my least favourite was bottle green.

It was raining when we docked, raining hard. We stood in silence watching the dockers make the ship fast. Everyone on shore was dressed in greyish muddy colours; the sky was grey, the bomb-scarred port was grey, shabby, dilapidated.

'Shall we get off last?' I wanted to put off the moment when I left the ship, my remaining link with India, and set foot on England.

'There's some sense in that. I'll go in the first rush and bag seats on the train and come back and get you.' Eagerly Dad went off to join the queue for the gangway.

So Mum and I and Clare stood under shelter and watched everyone tottering down the steep gangway, huddling their necks into their collars as they tried to keep the rain out. Some people laughed and flung their heads back, and drank in the fact it was English rain at last. One woman went down on her knees and kissed the wet quayside. Everyone ignored her.

Then it was our turn and I was glad of the rain because it hid the fact that I couldn't help crying as I left the old ship. Laden with our bags full of purchases made in Port Said – another world already – we followed Dad to the boat-train. The

81

station platform surprised me, it was so empty and clean. All my life I'd been used to Indian platforms where whole families lived, chattering or sleeping as they waited; where animals and even hens wandered and the sellers of tea or betel-nut or food shouted their wares. Here in Southampton the platforms seemed uncanny in their emptiness; the few people waiting for trains stood quietly in their dun-coloured macs and minded their own business.

I stared out through the rain-spattered window as the train pulled slowly out of Southampton and longed for India.

The sun came out as the train rushed towards London and a cheer worked its way up and down the carriages. The green, lush countryside looked even greener and I had to admit that England was beautiful. Blue sky was banishing the clouds and the sun was hot enough to make the wet roads steam. Everybody started walking up and down the boat-train, laughing and talking. We had all got to know each other, if only by sight, and here we all were for a final hour together, surrounded by sunny fields, sparkling streams and ponds and neat well-run farms. The whole train buzzed with people chatting and exchanging addresses and promising to keep in touch. Even Mrs Railton and Julie were pink and smiling; they insisted on giving us their address in Eastbourne.

It was strange, that train journey. It was like a mirage. Even I caught the excitement, the feeling that everything was right in the world, that adjusting to life in England was going to be easy, that Coming Home was indeed coming home. A mirage.

GUERNSEY

1

Why Not was galloping through the pine-woods ahead of the fire, but the trees became torches of solid flame in an instant. I hung on desperately, but Why Not was so frightened by the flames that she was tossing and bucking, trying to throw me off.

'Wake up, Nancy, wake up.' My mother was shaking me. 'Time to get up. We've arrived. Quickly.' At that moment the stewardess came and shouted that the gangways were down and would we get a move on please.

Sodden with sleep, upset by my dream, I got dressed and collected my stuff together for what seemed like the thousandth time since we started on our travels, and followed Mum and a whimpering Clare up to the disembarkation deck. Dad was already up there.

'Look, there's Sophie.' He pointed to some people standing on a flat-roofed viewpoint scanning our boat anxiously. I could see a very fat woman in a flowered dress and a tall one with red hair and glasses. I stared at them. I realized I was terrified of meeting Aunt Sophie.

'Sophie!' shouted Mum very loudly. 'Sophie!' And a thin woman in a blue guernsey and blue trousers and wellington boots suddenly started to wave madly back, smiling all over her face as much as Mum was.

Seagulls screamed endlessly round the mail-boat, hawsers and winches rattled and roared as the work of unloading the hold began. Cranes swung giddily above us as we came off the boat and were hugged by Aunt Sophie. The two sisters both cried and then laughed at their tears. Aunt Sophie looked like Mum, only ten instead of two years older. She was thin and her hair was grey; when she wasn't smiling at us her eyes looked hard and sad.

'I'll go ahead with Helen and the children and you can follow in a taxi with the luggage, Bernard, when it finally comes out of the hold. They always take a long time.'

'I'll stay with Dad,' I said quickly. We watched Sophie's Baby Austin crawl away from the harbour.

'That car's on its last legs. Come on, Nancy, let's look at the harbour while we wait. I always think St Peter Port is the best thing about Guernsey. So attractive. See, there's Castle Cornet.'

I looked at the castle guarding the harbour mouth, at the houses clustered along the sea-front and climbing the steep slopes behind.

'I'm hungry.' The Town Church clock told me it was just before seven.

'You should have gone with the others, then.'

Seagulls were fighting noisily over something that had been thrown into the sea. A boy of my own age was rowing a dinghy across the harbour; watched him moor the boat with quick practised fingers, then he picked up a basket containing his catch and climbed up the harbour wall on metal rungs before running off into the town.

Life in this island was clearly dominated by the sea.

2

'Robert Le Patourel has never come back. He disappeared after he was freed from the prisoner of war camp where he had spent four years,' said Dad.

Our taxi, laden with luggage, went very slowly. The driver had such a broad Guernsey accent I could hardly understand him. He crouched over the wheel, urging his old vehicle up the steep hills of St Peter Port. Dad had pointed out some horrible-looking iron gates in a tall granite wall which led to my new school.

'So is Uncle Robert dead?'

'No-one knows for certain, but I would have thought so. There has been absolutely no trace of him.'

'Perhaps he died in the camp.'

'Maybe. Poor Sophie has had to carry on, not knowing whether he's alive or dead. It's been very hard on her.'

We drove for what seemed like hours along narrow twisting roads. High banks, granite walls, big solid farmhouses of pink or grey granite; and greenhouses everywhere, the glass flashing in the early morning sun. The houses had a secret air, hiding in hollows with small, deep-set windows and arched front doors like the top part of a yawn.

Guernsey seemed like an island full of secrets and secrecy. I later discovered that the fronts of houses always looked closed and secret, mainly because they were unused. Nobody used their front doors, they all went round to the yard at the back. It couldn't have been more different from India, where everything happens more visibly and all doors are usually wide open.

By the time we finally arrived at the Le Patourels' house, I was so hungry I could think of nothing else. Maison de Haut was like many other farmhouses we had passed: tucked away from the main road, it fronted on a little lane, a long blue-grey granite house with an arched front door and lots of those secret-looking windows. The roof was of slate, not tiles, which increased the severe impression the house gave.

Beyond the house the lane dropped sharply downhill towards a great sweep of bay full of sand and rocks. Beyond the many jagged rocks was a little green island on the right; in the centre of the bay was a curiously familiar fort and way beyond the big point in the distance was the tiny spike of a lighthouse.

'Marvellous view, Nancy. And there's Fort Grey . . . remember our picture?'

As if I could forget. Poor picture, now ashes.

The taxi swung through granite gate-posts into the backyard, pulling up beside the Baby Austin. Aunt Sophie spoke to the driver in Guernsey French while Dad was digging the fare out of his pocket.

'I didn't know you could speak the patois,' said

Dad as we carried the luggage towards the back door.

'We all found it very useful during the Occupation,' said my aunt grimly. 'The Germans couldn't understand a word we said.'

The Occupation. All during my childhood the word 'occupation' had cropped up, whenever Red Cross messages arrived from Guernsey for my parents. The Channel Islands: the only part of the British Isles taken by the enemy. I used to find the word 'occupation' strange; if you were occupied you were busy, if a lavatory was occupied you had to wait. None of these meanings had much to do with war. I couldn't help being puzzled.

Nervously I followed Aunt Sophie into the dark kitchen. It was full of people, some sitting round the large table and some standing back in the shadows. Mum was sitting with Clare in her lap at the head of the table.

'Basil, Agnes, Marie, Pierre and there in the corner is Jean the cowman. Off you go, Jean, you've seen everyone now and it's time you saw to the cows instead.' Jean had about as many teeth as Bahyong and little rat-like eyes that darted about. He smelled of the cowshed.

'Right, breakfast for you both. I'm sure you're famished.'

I sat down beside my mother, as tongue-tied as all my cousins. Aunt Sophie put bowls of porridge in front of Dad and me, without asking us if we liked it. I didn't, but I was so hungry I gobbled it down anyway. My insides started to unclench.

'Bacon?' Agnes threw some pieces of bacon into a pan on the big black range and stirred them around. She was nineteen, with rather frizzy black hair and eyes close together in her long thin face. She smiled at me and for a moment looked really pretty. Basil, two years younger, was hacking slices of bacon off a big haunch on the draining board.

'Cut it thinner, Bas. That leg's meant to last us a good long time.'

'So rationing hasn't stopped you having big sides of bacon from the farm . . .' began Mum.

'This is black market,' said Basil. He was small for his age, with green eyes and brown hair like Mum's. In fact, there was a distinct family likeness. 'Strictly illegal.' He took the bacon and hung it up in a high dark cupboard behind some coats.

'We put a hat on it and no-one would know there was anything there that shouldn't be. We have to be careful because the inspectors are always coming round the farms to see you're not holding too much back.' Aunt Sophie sighed. 'You can't get away with much these days. It's almost as bad as when the Germans were here.'

The smell of frying bacon was divine. I couldn't listen any more to the conversation; I waited for Agnes to turn round with my bacon.

With another smile, she put the plate in front of me. The bacon was so good – rich tender meat and sweet delicate fat – that I could have eaten ten pieces instead of the one I was allowed.

As I ate, I was aware of my twin cousins, Marie and Pierre, watching me, but if I looked at them they immediately lowered their gaze. So I gave my perfect bacon my full attention until I'd savoured every morsel and then I looked around again. Marie and Pierre were sitting together at the end of the table. They were about fifteen, a year or so older than me. They had dark hair like Agnes and the same narrow face, but their eyes were like Basil's. They were very alike, yet not identical; they muttered to each other in undertones. Neither of them smiled at me once. When Jean the cowman finally shambled out of the kitchen, they slipped away after him.

The warm glow which breakfast had given me began to subside and disappeared altogether when Agnes took me upstairs to show me my room.

3

Stone-flagged hall, circular stone staircase. Hard grey granite. It was harsh and cold under my feet as I followed Agnes.

'You're sharing with Marie while we're so full. When your parents go back to India, you'll have this room to yourself, because they're in Marie's room.'

Upstairs were two long wood-panelled corridors and all the rooms leading off were divided by the same dark, almost black, oak panelling. Guernsey farmhouses are stone shells divided up inside with wood. The floors creaked, the rooms were very sombre by daylight with their small deep-set windows which let in little light. But at night these rooms were very cosy; you felt as if you were in a cave. If the wind roared outside, as it frequently did, the thick walls made you feel snug.

My room wasn't very big, and was even more

cramped because of Marie's camp-bed alongside mine. Agnes pulled open the wardrobe, a massive great thing covered with carvings, and said:

'Just as I expected, she's pinched all the hangers. And most of the shelves. Just push her stuff up, Nancy, take what space you need. I'll fetch you some more hangers.' Agnes smiled, this time the dutiful smile of an elder cousin to a shy lump. She went off down the reverberating corridor and came back with three hangers.

'This is all I can find. Let's double up some of Marie's clothes.'

'No, please don't . . . three hangers is plenty for the moment.' I didn't want to antagonize Marie any more than I needed to.

But Agnes went ahead and doubled up several hangers, saying as she did so that Marie was a selfish pig.

'Look. Just one blouse on this. She should have thought a bit.' I had a feeling Marie had thought and come to a different conclusion. Then Agnes smiled, her warm smile this time. 'I like your shoes, by the way. I've never seen any like that. Leather crossed over. Very pretty.'

'The Indians call them *chapplis*.'

'India. India. I really can't imagine what it's like.'

I stared at her across the dim bedroom and said: 'The light is so bright sometimes you can hardly see. You feel the sun is going to melt you away.'

'Wonderful,' said Agnes. 'I love the sun.' I noticed that her face and hands were brown, but since, like everyone else in the family, she wore a navy blue guernsey, the tan seemed to drain away against the dead blue colour. Then somebody called her and she hurried away. I sat down on my bed and wondered how on earth I was going to endure sleeping three feet away from an unknown cousin who didn't look as if she wanted me in the house at all.

Hanging in the wardrobe were a bottle green school tunic and blazer. Bottle green. Marie's uniform. Perhaps term had already started . . . what was today, a Saturday? I'd lost all sense of time.

On a small table in the corner of the room was a pile of exercise books with Guernsey Ladies' College stamped on them in gold above a gold shield with three lions on it. A gold scroll bore the words:

Fais ce que dois
Advienne que pourra.

French, I had done no French in Shillong. School was going to be a nightmare; perhaps they all spoke patois or real French all the time. Jabber, jabber, jabber. I felt sick.

I heard a noise of shouting and clattering outside in the lane and looked out to see Marie and Pierre driving off in a little dogcart harnessed to a donkey. They were urging the donkey to go faster, but it put its ears forward in disobedience and took no notice. They disappeared down the lane towards the sea.

A donkey. They had a donkey. I felt my heart lift a little.

'Isn't this a sweet room? I've always loved that Breton cupboard. Poor Marie, I do feel guilty she's had to give her room to us.' Mum had come in carrying luggage.

91

'You didn't tell me they had a donkey here.'

'They don't. It belongs to the farm next door. Marie and Pierre have gone to help collect vraic from the beach.'

'What's vraic?'

'Seaweed, to spread on the land as fertilizer.'

'Mum, I'm in despair over French.'

'Don't worry, you're to have private coaching until you catch up.' She looked at Marie's exercise books. 'I remember *fais ce que dois, advienne que pourra*. That means "do your duty, come what may."' Translated, the words sounded as cheerless as they had when they were a mystery. 'They haven't changed the colours of the exercise books since my day, either; still purple for scripture. Term has started, by the way. We're going to meet the headmistress on Monday and I expect you'll start school on Tuesday.'

'Can't I get used to Guernsey for a while first . . .'

But she didn't hear, because Dad and Basil were heaving luggage up the staircase and she went to help. I sat on the bed again. There was no escape from the horrible prospect ahead of me. In no time I would be encased in bottle green, doing my duty come what may.

4

'We must go and see Grand-père and Grand-mère this afternoon. And then if there's time we'll drop in on the Little Aunts.' Mum stood in the kitchen wearing a guernsey already and looking more and more like her sister Sophie by the minute. As she spoke there was the sound of a car in the yard; a bald man in dirty working clothes got out of it.

'Good Lord, it's John.' Aunt Sophie wore her grim expression. 'Brother John to see you, Helen. You should feel honoured. I've hardly seen him since the Germans left two years ago.'

My Uncle John was their eldest brother; he was fat, with slit green eyes and bundles of hair growing out of his nostrils and ears. Mum and Dad greeted him like a stranger; no-one was at ease. Aunt Sophie never turned round from the sink when she offered him a cup of tea, which he accepted with alacrity. I could see there was going to be a boring half hour ahead, so I managed to ease myself out of the kitchen into the yard.

I had no idea until today how many relatives we had in Guernsey. They were like an army, all waiting to meet us. I had eleven great aunts and uncles, to start with; one great uncle, Basil, had five children and seventeen grandchildren on the island. What an appalling spread of cousins just from him. Then there were the two great aunts known as the Little Aunts who were my grandfather's older sisters, Susannah and Laetitia. They lived together because they had never married – so no cousins to worry about there. And none from Uncle John either; his wife had left him years ago. And none from Uncle Abraham, but that was different.

My grandparents, Abraham and Esmée Queripel, had four children: John, Sophie, Helen and Abraham. Abraham was much the youngest and was killed in action in 1942. When Mum got the

Red Cross message she wept for hours. I had never seen her weep before and I sat numb and anxious on the veranda outside her bedroom waiting for her to stop.

Abraham, Basil, Laetitia . . . all these strange names, family names going back into a past so foreign to me. I wandered through the orchard behind Maison de Haut, looking for a nice windfall to eat. Wasps buzzed inside half-eaten apples all over the grass. I found one that had recently fallen and bit into it. My first English apple. All my life I had eaten big red apples from Kashmir, with sweet white flesh and big pips. Dad used to slice them on a plate when he had his morning tea and I'd eat my share as slowly as I could, they were so delicious.

This apple was quite different, sharp and strong with yellow flesh. As I ate it I went towards a big wall along one side of the orchard and climbed on top of it. Below me was the lane; down in the bay the sea twinkled in the sunshine. I longed to go down there, but I knew that the rest of today was to be spent visiting some of those relatives. It had been so different in Shillong; no-one in the whole of India was related to us. The people we knew were just friends. Here everyone seemed to be related to everyone; I felt as if I was caught in a spider's web.

There were footsteps in the lane and Basil appeared below me.

'Hullo, Nancy. Tell me, did I catch sight of Uncle John's car as I went past?'

'Yes.'

'Thought so. I'm off then, can't stand that man. Tell Mum I'm down at Le Puit.'

'Le what?'

'Puit. The farm down the lane there. P . . . u . . . i . . . t, pronounced pouee.'

'Why don't you like Uncle John?'

'He was a coward during the war and he collaborated with the Germans. I think those are good enough reasons, don't you?'

I stayed on the wall after he'd gone. It was becoming very clear to me that the German Occupation of Guernsey was still part of everyone's life and had left its stain everywhere.

'Nancy!' My father saw me through the trees and came and joined me on the wall.

'Dad, everybody keeps talking about the Germans. I don't even know what they did here, or how long they stayed. And Basil just told me Uncle John was a collaborator. What on earth did he do?'

'I don't know and I don't want to. It's better to put these things behind us. But what we mustn't forget is how very long the Occupation lasted and how difficult life was. The Germans arrived right at the beginning of the war, in June 1940, and they were here until May 1945. Food was very short, particularly at the end when the Channel Islands were literally starving; supplies of household goods ran out completely. Sophie said how precious things like needles and safety pins and cotton wool became. No soap, no toothpaste. No fresh fruit in winter unless you had your own supply of apples. And of course everybody stole your fruit; Sophie was saying that this orchard was a real headache to guard because people came over the wall at night and helped themselves. The thieves were usually German soldiers; they were as hungry as the islanders by the end.'

'Was Uncle Robert here in the occupation?'

'No, he'd joined up and was captured in France, I think. The bitterness about John is because he didn't join the army. So he was trapped here whether he liked it or not.'

'I didn't realize how much the war had hurt people here. It must be awful for my cousins not knowing where their father is, alive or dead.'

'See that greenhouse over there?' Dad pointed to a forlorn greenhouse with many broken panes of glass. 'Robert was obsessed with growing orchids, he had that greenhouse full of them. They must have all died.'

'What was he like?'

'Agnes is the one who looks most like him. He was a strange man, very moody. A bit unbalanced to tell the truth. I found him very difficult to get on with.'

'Dad, do I have to come this afternoon?'

'Of course. Your grandparents have never met you, or you them.'

'I know. But I'm dreading meeting so many relatives all at once, I really am. I'd rather go into a jungle full of tigers.'

Dad laughed and then we were both silent. I was back in the jungles of Assam; deep green secretive vegetation full of rustles and sudden noises filled my mind. I don't know what Dad was remembering, but his eyes were far away. We were deaf and blind to the sea wind, the gulls, the small green fields and the lush orchard around us.

5

Grandparents. Old age and cobwebs and black cats and whispers from rocking chairs. Instead I saw a tanned, white-haired man digging energetically in his front garden, throwing roots into a wheelbarrow.

'Dad. Dad!' My mother stood at the gate and the man turned slowly round. Then he gave a roar, threw his spade aside and opened his arms.

'Helen!'

I found it very strange to see my mother being hugged and told to stop crying, there was no need, by her own father. I hung back while Dad went up with Clare. My grandfather put his big nose and bushy black eyebrows near Clare as he said hullo and of course Clare promptly dug her face into Dad's shoulder and started to bawl. He just chuckled and turned his bright blue eyes – like mine? – to me.

'Nancy.' He held his hands out and took mine. 'Nancy. You won't cry if I kiss you, will you? I seem to have that effect on the others.' His cheek was raspy and he smelled of tobacco and earth. His blue eyes fixed on mine again. 'You look uncommonly like your Great Aunt Laetitia. Uncommonly.'

'She doesn't at all, Dad,' began my mother.

'Stand them side by side and see.'

Then the front door of the big cream-painted house opened and a small brown-haired woman exactly like my mother came out. Her face was old

97

and lined but her hair hadn't gone grey at all. She was wearing a very baggy brown dress. Mum ran to her, but didn't hug her in quite the same way she'd hugged her father.

'Mum. You've got so thin. But it's made you look younger.'

My grandmother kissed us all as if she was in a hurry to get it over. 'We all lost weight in the war. My stomach's shrunk. I can't eat much now. Oh Nancy and Bernard, I can hardly believe you're really here.'

'You look so well, both of you.' Mum put her arms round them. 'Don't they, Bernard?'

'Short commons never hurt anyone,' said Grand-père briskly. 'But it's not short commons today. Time for tea. I specially fetched some Guernsey gâche from Le Noury's this morning in your honour.'

The dining-room had dark striped wallpaper peeling off the walls in places, red velvet curtains that were old and faded and a huge mahogany table with matching chairs that were oozing horsehair stuffing from fat domed seats. There'd been a lot of talk about the wonders of gâche, but it turned out to be a sort of bready cake full of dried fruit. It looked dry and tasted dry; I fiddled with my slice until it disintegrated. Prickly horsehair was scratching my thighs. Conversations buzzed round me, about the Occupation, about Robert Le Patourel's disappearance, about our fire which of course no-one in Guernsey knew had happened. Grand-mère asked the question we had not stopped asking:

'How did it happen?'

'We'll probably never know. Arson, or one of

our oil lamps flaring up, who knows? It seemed to have started in the dining-room.'

'What a terrible thing. Lucky you didn't lose too much. I'm going to make a fresh pot. Eat up, eat up. Nancy, have one of those cakes, do.'

'You haven't eaten anything yourself, Mum,' said my mother in a rather barbed voice.

'I've had plenty.'

'You've had almost nothing.'

'The Germans took away my appetite.' Grand-mère went off to the kitchen with the teapot. My mother turned to her father.

'She's too thin, Dad. Much too thin.'

'Oh, I don't know.' Grand-père looked vague. 'She's all right.'

'She talks about food all the time but doesn't eat it.'

'We all got a bit obsessed by food during the Occupation, you know . . . you do if there's never enough of it. Esmée can't seem to shake the obsession off, but she will, she will. What she's finding harder to get over is Abraham's death. By the way, I'd love you to go through his old child-hood things sometime; see if there's anything you want to take for your children.'

My grandmother came back in and pressed more tea on us.

6

The basement was unused except for storage; room after dusty room, floored with big granite slabs, full of empty wine racks and old luggage and a broken rocking-horse. One room had a more organized air; I opened one of the many wooden boxes I found there and saw ranks of little lead soldiers. They'd been well-handled; the paint was rubbed off many. Abraham's soldiers, maybe John's before him. In another box was a train set and a great tangle of rails. On top was a mechanical tiger made of brightly-painted tin. It had a large rusty key fixed in its side; I picked the toy up and wound it as carefully as I could. Suddenly the tiger started thrashing its tail and opening and shutting its jaws with a grating noise a bit like a growl. I put it down on the stone floor and watched it with delight until it had wound down. Then I turned it over. On the underside of its belly were the words 'Made in India'. I wondered whether it had been a present from Mum to the brother so much younger than herself. Fifteen years younger . . . I remembered the photograph we'd had of him, standing on a rock by the sea, his thin arms in the air and a grin on his face as he prepared to launch himself off the rock. He'd been younger than me in that photo, about twelve.

It was such a lovely tiger in every way that I wound it up again. As I twisted the key carefully for the last little bit, to my horror there was a pinging sound and the tiger's mechanism died for ever. Feeling terrible, I put it back in the box full of trains and closed the lid.

'Nancy! Come upstairs now! We're off!'

I went upstairs steeling myself to confess I had broken Abraham's tiger, but Grand-mère gave me such a sweet smile when I appeared in the hall that I simply couldn't get the words out.

7

Our next and last call for the day was on the Little Aunts. I visualized two baby-sized aunts, but found that Great Aunt Susannah and Great Aunt Laetitia were only slightly shorter than me. They had blue eyes like their brother Abraham and soft white hair gathered into tight buns full of pins. Their dark dresses were almost to their ankles and their shoes had straps with shiny metal buttons. They smelled of powder and lavender, but their house smelled of cats. It was a strange little house in a narrow street high above St Peter Port, not far from my grandparents. The house was stuffed full of knick-knacks and photographs of the Queripel family. On every shelf there were china boots and shoes, hundreds of them, of all shapes and colours.

'It's my collection,' said Great Aunt Letty when she saw me pick up a white slipper with a mouse peeping out. 'I started it when I was your age. I have five hundred and twenty-three, counting the pairs as two. Mind you, I haven't got many pairs; they never make pairs as a rule.' She came close to me. Her blue eyes were faded as if someone had squirted milk in them.

So this was the aunt I was supposed to resemble. She had hairs sprouting from her chin, just a few, and bushy eyebrows like Grand-père's. Her nose was beaky and thin, but I could see that it was the same shape as mine; it had the same little bump at the end. Her teeth were yellow.

Great Aunt Letty was now cackling with laughter at something my father had said – my father looked like a giant in that room full of miniature objects. I watched her and felt suddenly sick with fear that this was what I might look like one day. It was an awful paralysing fear, a fear of growing old and ugly, of time passing without my being able to do anything about it.

'And how are Buttons and Alouette and Minette?'

'Ah, Buttons is dead. He died in 1941, he was eighteen you know. A good age for a cat.' Great Aunt Susannah's voice was much softer and gentler than her sister's. 'Alouette disappeared, we think the Germans ate her and Minette is still with us . . . you'll find her in the kitchen. Do you like cats, Nancy? Go and see her if you like. You'll find Winston there too.'

I escaped in the direction indicated. I just couldn't stay in the same room as Great Aunt Letty at that moment; I supposed I'd get used to the idea that I took after her, but it would take a while.

The kitchen was very dark and like a drawing in a Beatrix Potter book. Everything looked a hundred years old except the cats. A small black cat was sleeping in a chair and a huge fluffy grey cat was sitting impassively in the middle of the kitchen table. I decided this was Winston and began to stroke him. He purred very loudly and was so amiable he calmed my fears about looking like my great aunt.

'At least I'm going to be a foot taller than her,' I told him, 'for a start.'

Great Aunt Susannah tittupped down the tiled corridor into the kitchen and said immediately:

'Gracious, it's dark in here. There must be a storm brewing. Let me give you some light.' She lit a taper from a match and went over to a lamp on the wall. She held the taper to it as she turned a little lever and with a pop a mantle began to fill with light. I was fascinated; I'd never seen a gaslight before. My great aunt showed me how to light the other one. Then the black cat woke up and stretched.

'Ah, little Minette! She sleeps a lot, she's very old.'

At this point Great Aunt Letty came down the corridor to fetch the sherry and said:

'Goodness, lamps lit already. We don't need them yet,' and turned off the gas. The mantles dimmed slowly, as did the smile on Great Aunt Susannah's face.

8

Marie was sitting on my bed taking off her socks. They landed on the green lino with a soggy plop; they were soaked with sea-water and smelled like the ropes on the deck of the *City of Exeter*. She pushed them under the bed and started pulling on dry ones. I stood near the door, not knowing what to do. I'd already escaped from the kitchen as yet another relative dropped in to say hullo.

'Did you bring any sweets with you from India?' Marie looked up at me at last.

'We couldn't. Indian sweetmeats are very sticky and don't keep.'

'Don't they make toffee or boiled sweets?'

'Oh yes. Boiled sweets.'

'Pity you didn't bring some of those. Our sweet rations don't last a day.' Marie finished doing her shoes up and got off my bed.

'We didn't think of it.' Everyone had been very pleased with their presents, but we could easily have brought bagfuls of sweets as well.

'You wait until you have to manage on your ration. See this?' She took a printed yellowish-brown piece of paper out of her new purse and handed it to me. It had 'PERSONAL POINTS (SWEETS)' printed across the top and below that was her name: 'Marie Rose Le Patourel'. Below that were small squares marked with a letter and a number, E6, E6, E6, D6, D6, D6' on the top row, and 'E5, D5' etc. on the row below and so on. Some of these squares had been cut off. 'Each one of those is your week's ration of sweets or chocolate. The shopkeeper cuts them off when you've chosen what you want.'

'Do you have to pay for them as well?'

'Of course you have to pay for them.' Marie's scorn for my stupidity was clear. 'But however much money you have, you can't buy more than your measly ration. You'll get your ration book soon, I expect.'

'We should have brought a suitcase full of sweets for you all.' Marie sat down at the table in the corner and pulled her schoolbooks towards her.

'You've got a funny accent.'

'So have you.'

'Did you talk Indian all the time?'

I stared at her, unable to begin to convey to her the complexity of tongues I had heard even in my little corner of Assam.

'I talked Khasi to my ayah,' I said at last.

'Ayah?'

'Nurse; Clare and I shared her—'

'Nurse!' Marie gave a hooting whistle. 'Well, well.' I could feel myself getting annoyed. 'And what's *Kha* – what did you say?'

'Khasi. It's the dialect of the hillpeople where I lived.'

'Speak some now.' But I couldn't bring myself to use Khasi or Hindu words in this dark bedroom in an ancient Guernsey farmhouse near the sea. It didn't seem right. 'Go on, please speak some.'

I had a piercing longing for Congreeal, for her cuddly warm body smelling of betel-nut and hair oil and the spices she'd cooked with that day. I longed to be small again and be held close while she rocked me to make me feel sleepy and sang, as all ayahs sing to every baby:

> *Nini, baba, nini*
> *Roti makhan cini*
> *Roti makhan ho-gya*
> *Nini baba so-gya*

'Not now.' I went out and stood at the top of

the stone staircase in the dark. *Nini, baba, nini . . .*
all the song meant was:

> sleep, baby, sleep,
> bread, butter and sugar,
> bread and butter finished,
> sleep baby sleep.

Silly words, but they were the most comforting
in the world.

9

I wanted to walk by myself outside, but the way
out was through the kitchen and I couldn't face the
noisy chatter in there. I tried the front door, but it
was bolted with a huge rusting bolt I couldn't move.
There was a web with a busy spider in it across the
top right-hand corner of the door.

I retreated to the front parlour, a room off the
hall with a large granite fireplace and the usual low
black beams. It was furnished with heavy Victorian
pieces, upholstered in rich colours . . . red, dark blue,
green. In one corner was an upright piano, with
pretty inlays on the wood and candle sconces that
swung in front of the music stand. I tried some
notes; they were so out of tune that they sounded
like the half-tones Indian musicians use.

'Don't play the piano, Nancy, it upsets my
mother.' Basil stood in the doorway behind me. 'The
piano was Dad's, you see, he used to play it a lot.
She doesn't like to hear the sound of it in the house.'

As I closed the lid it slipped out of my fingers and banged. 'Sorry.'

'You can play it when she's out. I often do. It needs tuning, though.' He smiled at me, his green eyes kind. I liked Basil. 'Did you play in India?'

'No. I've never done any music. I can't read it either. Another of my gaps.'

'I've just bought an accordion, second-hand but a good one. Do you want to see it?'

I knew Basil was just being kind to me because he'd seen my face when he stopped me playing the piano, but all the same I felt myself cheer up as I followed him to his room. It was tucked away on its own over the kitchen. We could hear the talk easily through the floorboards.

Basil took his red and gold accordion out of a cupboard and slung it round his shoulders. He squeezed air into it and played a jazzy tune.

'I'm not very good yet. Luckily my friends don't mind.'

'You sound good to me.'

'A whole gang of us have started a night club in a barn and I play it there. If you shut your eyes, you think you're in Paris.' He grinned at me as he went on playing. Agnes stuck her head round the door.

'Bas – oh, hi, Nancy. Bas, are you going to the club tonight?'

'Fred's coming for me any minute.' With a loud squeeze of notes he silenced the accordion and did up various straps and catches.

'Can I cadge a lift?'

'What's happened to Neville then?'

'He had a close encounter with a granite wall.' Agnes looked rueful. 'His father's furious.'

'I bet.' Basil combed his hair, then picked up a packet of cigarettes and a lighter. 'Damn, these are nearly finished.'

'Have mine.' Agnes tossed a packet with Bucktrout printed across it on to the bed. 'If you ever need cigarettes, Nancy, just let me know. I work at Bucktrout's and they give me lots of extra packs as part of the pay.'

'I don't smoke.' I'd noticed everyone else seemed to.

'You will soon enough. Basil, wasn't that a car hooting?'

'That'll be Fred. Come on, let's go.' Accordion slung over his shoulder, he went to the door.

'Basil, can I stay in your room for a while?'

'In here?' Basil looked surprised. 'It's such a mess.'

'Pity we can't take you to the club with us.' Agnes smiled at me. 'Another couple of years and there'll be no holding you.'

The car horn sounded again, several times in succession.

'Bye, Nancy. Come on, Agnes.' He went, but Agnes paused at the door. 'Marie and Pierre haven't upset you, have they?' I shrugged. 'You mustn't let them worry you. The trouble is, they're not very friendly to other people because they've always had each other. They got worse when they were evacuated during the war. And since they've come back Mum's been so worried about everything she's let them do as they like.'

When they'd gone I sat on the deep window-sill

and looked out into the orchard. The trees were dark against the sunset; bats flew about. I sat feeling very peaceful; even the murmur of voices from below didn't spoil the peace. In fact, it made it better because I was alone and they weren't.

I was swinging, swinging through the jungle; I knew the Horseshoe Falls were below me because I could hear them and I could hear Bruce shouting that he was going to jump. I was swinging on a creeper that was so long I couldn't see the branch it was anchored to; I was swinging high and as the creeper took me back into the thick of the trees I saw fire, sheets of fire eating away the trunks.

'Jump, Nancy,' Bruce was shouting, 'jump'. Then the creeper broke and as I sailed through the air I knew I was going to land in the Falls; people were shouting as I rushed for ever through the air, then the water was pummelling me around—

'Wake up Nancy, wake up! We've been looking everywhere for you, we couldn't think where you'd gone. Didn't you hear us shouting?' My mother was holding an oil lamp in the dark unfamiliar room. It threw shadows that seemed still to be part of my dream. I tried to sit up.

'I feel sick.'

'And there's a power cut. Come on, Nancy, get up. What were you doing in Basil's room anyway?'

'He asked me in.' I sat on the edge of the bed.

'It's suppertime. Come on, everyone's waiting for you.' I could hear the buzz of conversation from downstairs.

'Mum, I feel awful. I couldn't eat anything. I just want to go to bed.' My mother felt my forehead and then put her arm round me. I stared at the bright juddering flame of the lamp and collapsed against her. 'I keep getting bad dreams,' I whispered. 'Dreams about fire.'

'So do I. But it's hardly surprising.'

I was filled with the pain of loss. 'Mum, I can't bear to think that our house is gone. I mind more since we stopped travelling.'

'I do too,' she whispered. We held each other tightly, our eyes shut now against the lamplight.

10

The headmistress of the Guernsey Ladies' College, Miss Porrit, had tiny ankles below bulging calves. She wore a purple dress, as stiff as a carpet, and her hair was cut short like a man's. Her eyes glared stiffly at you from deep in her head, even when her mouth was smiling. I didn't like her and I don't think she liked me.

'I've never had a Nancy at the college before. Not a usual name.' She was holding a piece of paper that I recognized: it was my most recent report from Pinemount School. 'Your last headmistress seems to think highly of you. I see you were top of your class, a class of let me see, ah yes, eleven girls. Well done.' I'd never heard anyone say well done with such a lack of enthusiasm. 'However, you're going to find a big difference here. The classes are double the size for one thing . . .'

'And I've done no French.'

She looked up sharply. 'I'd rather you didn't

110

interrupt, Nancy. Girls are encouraged not to interrupt at this school. Yes, no French. And I suspect your mathematics is going to be a problem too, from your efforts in our little test.'

Miss Porrit smiled; my mother laughed nervously and my father stared blankly out of the window at the crowds of girls in bottle green milling around the playground.

I don't know why horrible women like Miss Porrit are put in charge of schools. My headmistress in Shillong was a perfect sort of teacher: she encouraged you to talk to her, she listened and was interested, she knew and liked everybody. She gave the impression that we were all special to her. And she had no favourites; as soon as I met Miss Porrit I knew she'd be the sort to have favourites and I was right. We met one of them that day.

'I'm sure you'd like to see round the school, so I've arranged for one of your classmates, Renée Ferbrache, to take you over it.' Renée was neat and tidy and full of polite smiles. Miss Porrit beamed at her. 'Renée is the star of our inter-collegiate gymnastics team.'

Renée lowered her eyes with a little smile and led us away to see the hall, the gymnasium, the library. We tramped up and down creaking wooden staircases and girls stared at us. Mum was wearing a striking dress in Indian paisley cotton which was drawing every eye, as were my *chapplis*. I heard someone whisper to Renée on a staircase:

'Is that the girl from India? She doesn't look like an Indian at all.'

I wanted to laugh. I hadn't realized it before, but lots of people were going to assume that because

I'd been born and brought up in India, I must have Indian blood.

'I don't believe it, but yes . . . it *is* Helen Queripel-that-was!' cried a teacher who'd stopped in her tracks as we went by.

'Jackie Naftel!' While they kissed and chatted, Dad and I drifted on towards the school gates.

'All her old friends here refer to your mother as Helen Queripel-that-was. It used to annoy me, but I've got used to it. Though I'd prefer Helen Sykes-that-is.'

'No-one could mistake Sykes for a Guernsey name. Or Nancy. I hope I'm not going to be the only person at the college with an English name.' We stopped and waited: Mum was still excitedly talking. 'I didn't like Miss Porrit, Dad.'

'I didn't like her much either. But we're told she's a good headmistress who's pulling standards up all round.'

'I can't help thinking about Pinemount and Mrs Neal.'

'You're to stop comparing everything with Assam, Nancy. You'll make yourself miserable that way.'

I am miserable about the college already, I wanted to say, but I kept silent. Mum came running up and we headed for the Town.

11

Smith Street, The Pollet, Bordage, Berthelot Street, Fountain Street, Mill Street, the Arcade, the Market

. . it was all going to become so familiar. From the first moment I walked round it, I loved St Peter Port.

loved its steep narrow streets lined with smooth grey granite, I loved the way you saw the sea and the harbour through narrow little gaps as you walked down the High Street. The gaps contained steep flights of steps down to the quay, steps that often turned and ducked under buildings and emerged somewhere surprising. There were equally steep flights up to higher levels of the town, but these were less alluring. The town smelled of boats and rotting seaweed at low tide; at high tide the water sometimes lapped over the esplanade. You could often hear the rattle of cranes and, all the time, the crying of gulls.

'And now for your uniform. What a good thing Sophie got your ration book organized in advance.'

'I didn't know *clothes* were rationed too.'

'It's hard, isn't it? Specially when you have to spend it on uniform.'

'Oh God, bottle green.'

'Don't say oh God like that, and bottle green is very smart.'

'If it suits you.'

'Of course it'll suit you, you don't look that bad in green. Stop being perverse, Nancy. You and I are going to enjoy this little shopping spree; that's why I banished Bernard.' My father absolutely hated shopping and had gone off to look at Castle Cornet.

Even Mum's enthusiasm waned when she saw the acre of bottle green that had to be put on to my back to make me into a College girl. The worst things were the thick bottle green knickers we had to wear; they were enormous, baggy and had elastic round the tops of the legs so that you looked as if you were wearing knickerbockers. The next worst thing was the beret. It sat on my head like a solid green mushroom. I was supplied with a badge to be sewn on the front of it, a badge bearing the inevitable words, *Fais ce que dois, advienne que pourra.*

'Do I have to wear this beret all the time?' The sales lady obviously didn't approve of my total lack of enthusiasm for my uniform.

'You're lucky to be going to the College. My daughter tried for a scholarship but she didn't get it.' I kept quiet while she and my mother went through incredibly complicated transactions with clothing coupons. It looked as if I wouldn't be able to get any new clothes for years. Then the sales lady folded each garment with meticulous care, knickers included, and wrapped the lot in a huge sheet of sweet-smelling brown paper and tied it up with string.

'We must hurry down to the bus station. Bernard will be waiting for us by now.' I clutched the big crackling parcel as I hurried after my mother down Fountain Street. An alluring parcel, that should have been full of promise. As we drew near the harbour's edge and started looking around for Dad, I had a sudden wild desire to throw the parcel into the water.

'I see your shopping expedition was successful. Let me carry that enormous parcel for you, Nancy,' and my father with his usual good manners took the parcel from my itching fingers. Then we caught a bus, painted in shades of grey, which went very slowly and took a long long time to get us to St Peter in the Wood.

12

'Try my old bike,' said Agnes. 'It's yours now. Get used to it and then you can bike to school. I used to hate those buses.' She had fetched a rusty old bike from a shed and pumped up its tyres for me. 'The chain sometimes comes off, but it's easy to get back on.'

I wanted to go down to the sea and Agnes said I couldn't get lost if I just headed down the lanes towards it, though she advised me to return the long way round via the main road because coming back through the lanes was confusing if you didn't know exactly where you were heading.

It was a cool scudding day; white clouds raced across the sky like great fat sheep. Rocquaine Bay was spread before me as I raced downhill . . . the right-hand beach was called L'Eree and off its point was the small island of Lihou; the left-hand end was called Pleinmont and far off the point was the Hanoi lighthouse. Sand was being blown by the wind against outcrops of rock above the high water mark; the tide was sliding away leaving hard wet sand which the wind could not stir. I took the bike down a causeway and rode along the firm ridged sand. A group of boys who'd been swimming ran past me, their skins mottled red and blue in the cold wind which blew so stiffly into my face it nearly took my breath away.

When I came off the beach at the far causeway I decided to explore the headland beyond. I struggled against the wind with my eyes watering, wondering how anyone could go swimming for pleasure in such weather. The boys were now playing football and their shouts came faintly against the wind. Greenhouses inland winked in the sun. There was hardly anyone about.

When I reached the point I saw a large notice warning the public that since access to Lihou Island was only at low tide, they should take care not to get cut off. There were the remains of a stone building on the flat grass-covered island, but nothing else. I remembered my mother telling me about a Venus pool on the far side which was good for swimming and diving; you certainly couldn't have swum comfortably off the island, because it was edged all round with viciously sharp, red granite rocks.

The tide was beginning to uncover a causeway made of huge granite blocks like stepping stones. I was about to turn away when I saw a figure appear from behind the ruined building and walk along a grassy path. Perhaps someone had been cut off . . . but this man didn't look at all distressed. An animal bounced into view and followed the man. A goat? Then the two of them went round an outcrop of rock and disappeared from sight. I was alone again. A splash of rain hit my face. The tide was dropping so fast that almost as I watched more jagged granite teeth showed themselves through the churning sea.

I bicycled on round the headland; there was a rather ugly dispirited little bay on the other side, full of pebbles and long heaps of decaying seaweed. I was beginning to love the iodine-salty smell of the beach and the endless sound of the waves reminded me of the crashing waterfalls around Shillong.

It was only as I puffed up the long hill to Maison de Haut that I remembered the bottle green uniform and the fact that I had to wear it to school tomorrow.

13

'Does anyone live on Lihou Island?'

'Not any more.' Aunt Sophie was clattering pots and pans on and off the stove as she dished up.

'I saw a man and a goat – it looked like a goat – on it while the tide was still high.'

'Oh, people are always getting cut off. They never realize how fast the tide comes up. No, it's deserted now. There used to be a monastery on Lihou, or was it a nunnery, I forget. The Germans shot the old building to bits during the war with the big guns near here, at Le Frie Baton.' She put down the saucepan she was holding. 'That place was amazing, Helen. I went to look at it soon after the Germans were gone. I didn't realize there were four huge guns there, each over fifty feet long. I thought there was just one. Pierre looked tiny running up and down them. The Germans had disguised the base of each gun to look like a bungalow, with painted doors and windows and even painted curtains in the windows! When the barrel was lowered and covered with camouflage netting all you could see was this innocent-looking bungalow.' Aunt Sophie's eyes were flashing. 'You couldn't help admiring the effort they'd put into it.

From the air no-one could have told the difference between those bungalows and real ones. The stupid thing was that those guns may have looked impressive – they were supposed to have a range of forty miles – but most of the time their shells never got further than poor old Lihou! Giants with no power. Here, Nancy, take this oven cloth and help me put the dishes on the table.'

The family started to talk as they often did about the Germans. Clare enjoyed the hubbub of a noisy family meal and banged her spoon on the table and crowed. But I always found mealtimes difficult; I didn't know what to say, I wasn't used to the shouting and interrupting; as a result I hardly ever opened my mouth, except to eat, when I was at table. I overheard Pierre calling me, 'our little Indian mouse'. It hurt but what could I do? They weren't interested in me, I didn't have anything much to contribute; anything I said had about as much effect as a stone dropped into a pool.

'You're going to have a lovely time with all your cousins, I can see.' Mum was giving Clare her bath and I'd joined them. Clare was sitting in a tin tub, rubbing soap all over her round fat stomach and then rinsing it off with water poured from the brown bakelite soap-dish which to her was a boat, a fish, a perfect toy. In-between the repeated soaping and the pouring she'd drink from the dish and smack her lips as if it tasted wonderful.

'It makes Dad and me feel happier about leaving you . . . at least you'll be part of a big happy family.'

'They're not very happy.'

'What makes you say that?' Clare started to pour

water on to the floor and Mum took the soap-dish away from her.

'They're haunted by their father.'

'Well, I think everyone's remarkably cheerful considering. Of course Sophie suffers the most, but she's very good at hiding it.'

I thought of the grim look on my aunt's face and her deadened eyes, and didn't feel she was good at hiding her pain. But perhaps Mum had expected her to be more upset, so I said nothing.

'I'm sure you'll become good friends with Marie.'

'She's not very friendly. She hardly talks to me in our room.'

'She's shy and so are you. It'll be easier when you've got your own rooms.'

'She and Pierre take no notice of anyone.'

'I expect it's because they were away for those five years, so they had to rely on each other.'

'Why weren't they all evacuated together?'

'Sophie didn't want to leave the house empty and Basil and Agnes refused to go. Marie and Pierre had each other so they were easier to persuade. It must have been awful for Sophie to see them go. A ship-load of children going off into the blue for God knows how long. At least we *know* how long we're leaving you. Those two years will fly past, you'll see.'

Clare was standing up, trying to reach the soap-dish. Her bottom had a red line across it to mark the water-level.

'Clare will be nearly four when I see her again.' I pressed my face to Clare's warm squirmy back to hide the fact I was near to crying.

'And you'll be sixteen.' Mum busied herself

119

round the bathroom, the way people do when they're feeling upset and don't want to show it. I blew bubbles into Clare's bathwater with a piece of rubber piping.

She screeched with delight and shouted for more, splashing water everywhere. Bubbles rumbled round her fat stubby legs.

'Sixteen.' I looked up and saw Mum standing stock still in the middle of the bathroom. 'Sixteen and nearly grown-up.'

'I think I'm going to be permanently infantile. Marie obviously thinks I am. She treats me as if I'm about ten. Or less.' I blew another batch of noisy bubbles for Clare and then gave her the pipe to try doing it herself.

'Well, I suppose in a sense you are quite—'

'Young for my age. I wish you'd stop saying that. And I wish I knew what being old for my age felt like.'

Clare dropped the pipe on the floor and held up her hands. I picked her up, all wet and pink and cuddly.

'You'll know soon enough.'

'Will I? Other people seem to know whether you are or not . . . all you know yourself is that you're you.'

'True enough.' Mum was looking at me with a new expression in her eyes, almost as she'd looked when she first saw my new haircut in Bombay. Clare snuggled up close to me, cocooned in the towel.

'Never forget, Nancy, that I'm going to miss you dreadfully. Nothing is going to make up for the fact that for two years I won't see you at all.'

'Let me come back with you then.' But as I said it, I knew I didn't mean it and Mum knew I didn't. We smiled at each other over Clare's head.

'I honestly wish we could.'

It was the best conversation I'd ever had with my mother.

14

I went downstairs in my bottle green tunic, my badly-knotted tie, my stiff new shirt and my bottle green knickers which felt thick and baggy as a nappy. I'd lived my life in little briefs made by Ahmed out of the softest cotton; he'd always added some pretty extra detail . . . coloured stitching or cut-outs of fruit or animals made from bright scraps of cloth. A favourite pair, long since worn out, had a monkey swinging by its tail from a branch. I'd come to Guernsey with a dozen of Ahmed's briefs – the latest only had decorative stitching as befitted my advancing age – and now I'd have to spend most of my week in these ghastly green affairs.

I couldn't eat any breakfast, I was so nervous. I put my packed lunch of marmite sandwiches, a tomato and an apple into my sweet-smelling new leather satchel which otherwise only contained a pencil case, and followed Marie up the lane with Aunt Sophie calling behind us:

'Take her straight to Miss Porrit's office when you arrive, no messing about in the playground first, Marie . . .' Marie rolled her eyes and hurried on. We stood in silence at the bus-stop, until she pointed down to the shoreline of L'Eree and said:

'There's the bus and it's late. It should be up here by now.'

My stomach began to churn; I knew Miss Porrit wouldn't approve of lateness on the first day, my fault or not. Pierre bicycled past at that moment; he and Marie usually biked together. She hadn't been too pleased to be switched to the bus just for my benefit.

'You're going to be late,' called Pierre cheerfully.

'Thanks a lot, we know.'

'I'm sorry they wouldn't let me bike with you today.'

Marie must have noticed at last how miserable I was, because she softened.

'It doesn't matter if we're late. I'll stick with you and make sure old Porrit knows it wasn't your fault. That woman can be such a pig.'

'You'll find us a very friendly school,' Miss Porrit said, her eyes ice-cold above her smile. 'Don't look so nervous. I'll take you to your classroom myself.' She said this as if she was conferring a great honour on me. I followed her solid slightly creaking body, encased today in sludgy yellow, and tried deep breathing. She flung open a door and a teacher who looked like a robin – brown, small, with a red jersey – stopped taking the register.

'This is Nancy Sykes, Miss Brackenbridge, the new girl from India.'

The whole class gazed in silence at me. I wanted to die. I somehow found myself sitting at a desk in the second row, staring down at all the carved initials in its lid while Miss Brackenbridge finished the register.

'Liza Le Pelley, Diana Le Tissier, Susanne Martel, Stella Marquand, Joanne Naftel, Marjorie Ozanne, Susan Short, Angela Thoumine, Olive Tozier, Erica Upton.' She looked up and smiled at me. 'And now we must add Nancy Sykes. Nancy, I think the best thing is for your neighbour Ann de Garis to look after you today. Take her straight to the stationery office after assembly and make sure she gets everything she needs, Ann. And then, Nancy, you must copy up your timetable as soon as you can.'

I knew that the next couple of hours would be bearable: I was being safely drawn into the dull school routine. What I was dreading was my first break. I had often found breaks an ordeal even at Pinemount School, where I'd known the other children well. When I saw a large number of people surging about and shouting I felt myself going cold at the edges.

The bell rang for break. The cloakroom was in chaos: the noise in the other lavatories was deafening . . . doors banged, voices echoed and the flushes made an extra loud noise if you could pull them at all. I must have pulled mine ten times before anything happened. I could hear Ann giggling outside as she waited for me. I longed to stay locked in the lavatory throughout break, unpleasant though it was in there.

'This is my friend Betty Bougourd.'

I knew as soon as Betty Bougourd smiled at me that she was not going to be a friend of mine. Her smile was like a sneer; she had frizzy blond hair,

123

top teeth that stuck out and a large mole on one earlobe.

'Hullo, Nancy Sykes from Indeeah. We didn't expect you to be paler than us.'

'In India you keep out of the sun.' But oh for that sun, that dazzling blinding sun . . .

'Come out and meet our gang. We're on the tennis-courts.'

I had to follow Ann and Betty out on to that dizzy-making playground because I could see no alternative. I focused my eyes on Ann's brown plaits and followed her as blindly as I could. She and Betty led me to a group of ten or so girls sitting on the grassy corner of a tennis-court. Betty was obviously the leader of the group and she introduced them to me in such a joky mocking way that I hardly took in a name. Except for one: Stella Marquand. Betty didn't joke about Stella, so I gathered from her offhand tone that Stella wasn't really part of the gang.

But Stella was the one I took to. She had a thin face, red hair and a rather deep abrupt voice. She started to move away from the group soon after I'd been introduced to her. I made a split-second decision and followed her; I could sense Betty's eyes on my back.

'Tell me about the College,' I said. I couldn't think of anything else to say that might make her stop and talk.

'OK.' We sat down against a wall, about twenty feet from the other group. 'What do you want to know?'

I asked her some boring questions and she answered them, but neither of us was really paying much attention to what we were saying. We were taking in who we were. Stella had alert yellowish-green eyes and dark brows; she opened her eyes wide and fixed them on you when she was saying anything. After the shifting, secretive eyes of my cousins, it was refreshing.

'And finally, take no notice of Miss Porrit. I actually think she's a sadist. She gets at everyone except her favourites and since you don't look cut out to be one, just keep your head down when she's around.'

'So *there* you are, Stella. I've been looking everywhere for you.' A tall girl, even taller than Stella, stood crossly in front of her. She had such a long gym slip on she looked a bit like a tree.

'Help. I completely forgot. Sorry, Marion. This is Nancy . . .'

'Well, come now. It's not too late. Hullo.' She added this in my direction as she dragged Stella away.

I sat there alone until the bell went five minutes later and then tagged along beside Ann de Garis.

'So our Stella just left you high and dry, did she?' said Betty Bougourd with relish. 'Typical.'

15

By the end of the day, I knew that the one person in that class I wanted for a friend was Stella Marquand. She and her friend Marion Evans sat at the back of the room and talked a lot together, to Miss Brackenbridge's annoyance. Miss

Brackenbridge was obviously hopeless at keeping order – this was a relief. I'd been expecting all the teachers to be as awful as Miss Porrit, who wouldn't have allowed a yawn to escape, let alone a whisper.

I sat alone in the bus going home and brooded on my day. I'd told Marie I could manage to ride home on my own, I remembered the stop. She was relieved and gave me a very nice grin when she said thanks, that suited her because she wanted to go down to the Town after school. I'd seen Stella and Marion heading downhill for the Town, laughing together, as I turned uphill for my bus. They were clearly best friends; they'd probably known each other for years. I felt depressed. I was the total outsider.

I was so deep in my thoughts as the bus chugged along that I missed my stop. I only realized what I'd done when the bus stopped going downhill and I saw the coastline of L'Eree ahead of me. First I panicked and then I decided that if I got out at the edge of the beach, I could walk up to Maison de Haut through the lanes.

The trouble with Guernsey lanes is that they all look alike and they twist and turn. You can never tell which is the most direct just by looking at it. I could see Maison de Haut up on the hill when I started up what I thought was the lane I'd taken yesterday, but quickly it began to offer me turnings I didn't remember. By this time I was so deep in the winding lanes that I could no longer see the house above me. I turned left, I turned right. At least I was still going uphill, I said to myself, and then the lane I was in did a great bend to the right and downhill it went with no signs of returning. I retraced my steps and took another turning; if I'd seen someone I'd have asked the way, but the lanes were deserted. The few cottages I passed looked shut and secretive; I knocked on one door but got no reply.

I was beginning to feel desperately lost when I saw the name Le Puit on a gate in a high granite wall. Then I remembered: Basil was always going down to Le Puit. Relieved, I pushed the gate open; maybe Basil himself was here.

The big granite farmhouse, grey like ours, had larger windows and a red front door. I knocked and nothing happened. By now I was beginning to see that no-one used their front doors; this one was probably as sealed up as the one at Maison de Haut.

The yard at the back was littered with broken old farm machinery. Hens were sitting contentedly on the heaps of rusty metal. There was churned mud everywhere and a series of barns and sheds with open doors. I was about to pick my way towards one of them when a row of mooing cows plodded into the farmyard followed by a wild-looking man with a battered green hat and almost no front teeth.

'Wait a minute, eh,' he shouted at me in a rich Guernsey accent. 'Let me get these buggers into the milking shed and I'll be with you. Just hang on right where you are.' So I stood in the mud in my neat school uniform and waited while the man cursed and shouted at his cows. Then he came out of the shed, beaming at me. 'I know who you are, my girl. You're a Queripel through and through. You'll be Helen's girl back from India. Want a drink of milk straight from the cow? Come with me, then. I'm Ted Guillemette, by the way.'

'Nancy Sykes. You guessed right.'

'Flo! Give us a cup for this young lady. My wife, Florence. This is Helen's eldest.'

'I knew without being told. Hullo, Nancy.' Flo Guillemette was sitting on a stool, milking. She grinned at me as she pulled at the udders; unlike Ted, she had a row of huge white teeth like a horse's. Her hands moved with a quick easy rhythm as the milk purred into the churn. 'Switch the churn then and give her some, Ted.'

So I tasted my first fresh milk, still foaming, straight from a large lugubrious cow called Queenie, who flicked her tail at me and chewed the cud. The smell of cow and sweet milk and soaked concrete filled the shed; deafening clatters and bangs came from an adjacent dairy where someone was washing out the large metal churns.

'Bas!' called Ted. 'We've got a visitor.' And Basil came out of the dairy in a long rubber apron and wellingtons.

'Nancy . . . what brings you here?'

'I got lost walking up from L'Eree. I saw the name Le Puit and came in to ask the way.'

'You walk her up, Bas, if you've finished rinsing out those cans.'

'I thought Marie was looking after you today?'

'I told her I could manage. Really, it was my fault I missed the stop.' Basil grunted and went off to the dairy.

'So how was the first day at school, eh?' Ted seemed to know a lot about me.

'Better than I expected.'

'I never could abide education. And there's me with a son who has his nose in a book twenty-four hours a day.'

'He's just compensating,' came Flo's voice from almost under the cow.

'I may have left school at fourteen but cor dammee, my brain's fine.' Everyone in Guernsey kept saying dammee or cor dammee, just as they said chirree for cheerio. 'Chirree, you two. *A la prochaine.*'

As we walked up the lane Basil told me about the Guillemettes. 'Old Ted was in charge of reporting the milk yield to the Germans during the Occupation. He led them a right dance, drove them crazy. They were sure he was cheating them, but they could never prove it. Then Flo hid a British airman for weeks until some bastard betrayed her. She had to do a spell in prison in France, poor thing. Their son Edmund was evacuated to England during the war and found himself living with a professor's family. He's become a real egghead; he was always good at maths and now he's got into Cambridge. No-one in their family has ever gone to university.'

'Is he there now?'

'Next year. Ah well. Before he went away we were best friends, now we don't seem to have much in common. Edmund's the only child and I know Ted's sad he isn't interested in the farm.'

'So the war changed his life, too.'

'The bloody war changed all our lives.' Basil's voice was bitter. 'All our lives.' I knew how unpleasant it was to have your life changed against your will, but I couldn't bring myself to say it. Basil stopped. 'There's a row going on. Listen.'

From somewhere just inside the gateway of

Maison de Haut we could hear a tirade in my aunt's voice.

'You just do what you damn well please all the time. You're supposed to be looking after your cousin and what do you do? You go off into the town with your friends and waste your time and forget all about her. Well, let me tell you my girl, Nancy's not back yet and I don't know where she is.' I was about to run forward, but Basil put his finger to his lips and held my arm. 'Did she get the bus straight after school?'

'I don't know—'

'So you didn't even have the kindness to see her on to the bus.'

'She said she could manage. It's not that difficult, Mum—'

'It's not a question of whether it was difficult or not. It's a question of doing what you were asked to do and of kindness to a cousin. I'm ashamed of you, I really am.'

Basil suddenly leapt out, dragging me behind him. Marie and Aunt Sophie were standing gazing furiously at each other; their faces went blank with surprise when they saw us.

'Here she is, safe and sound,' said Basil and added as he strolled past Marie: 'Well done, sister.' Marie gave me a hard glance before she picked up her satchel and followed her brother round the house. Aunt Sophie watched her with a stony, grim expression which I found a bit frightening.

'It was my fault, honestly. I knew where to get out but I was daydreaming and missed it.'

'It was Marie's fault. She just pleases herself. She's been spoiled rotten and not by me.'

'I told her I wanted to return on my own.'

Aunt Sophie turned away, her expression still steely, and went back to her weeding. Upset, I went round the house.

There in the back-yard was Clare, trying to catch a hen. The hen, known as Mrs Tick Tock, was very tame; she stood quite still staring eye to eye at Clare. Clare made a grab and Mrs Tick Tock surprised her by sitting down. So Clare started patting her instead and I joined her. My mother was sitting on the mounting block in the late afternoon sun, mending something.

'Hullo, darling.' She obviously thought I'd come back with Marie after all. 'How was school then?'

I began to tell her when Dad appeared and asked me the same question. I feared it was a question I'd be asked tediously often. But answering put off the moment I knew would come, when I had to go and change and face Marie. I was at the top of the stone stairs when a door banged and Marie came rushing down the corridor towards me. When she saw me she froze.

'You certainly are a bringer of trouble,' she hissed as she pushed past me. I tried to say sorry but she'd already gone into Pierre's room and banged that door too. I went and flung myself on my bed, too fed up even to take off my uniform.

The only advantage in my parents going back to India was that I'd then have a room to myself.

16

As September turned to October there were weeks of golden serene weather. The clear light in the morning reminded me of the cold weather in India for a minute or two, but was really quite different. The sun seemed smaller. There were the sights and smells of an unfamiliar autumn all around me: leaves turning brown and dropping, misty bonfire smells, scents of moss and rotting fallen leaves. Assam was full of evergreen trees; here it was strange to see the bare branches above me and lovely to drag my feet through deep drifts of leaves. The great oozing heaps of exhausted tomato plants recently torn out of greenhouses gave off their own peculiar smell. The salty yet sweetish scent of seaweed decaying on the fields was constantly in the background in the lanes around Maison de Haut.

I bided my time during this halcyon weather. At school I paid attention and watched the other girls and waited to see if Stella would shake herself loose from Marion Evans one day. I worked hard to catch up with the subjects I was weak in and my father helped to explain things I didn't understand. I avoided confrontations with Marie and she with me. She bicycled in to school with Pierre, I took the bus for the moment.

Then suddenly the weather broke and the first big storm of the winter hit us, blowing with all the power of the Atlantic behind it. Biting winds, stinging rain, black clouds. It was so dark in Maison de Haut at midday that it seemed like night. Dark, dark, dark, with grey granite, blue granite somehow absorbing what light and warmth there was. The house was unheated except for the large kitchen range. In the evenings a fire was lit in the sitting-room and when it got really cold there were a couple of oil stoves standing on tin trays in the stone-flagged hall, smelling of paraffin and blackened wicks as they gave off a minimal heat. I felt cold to the marrow of my bones.

At school it was just as bad. The heating was provided by a big fearsome-looking boiler in the hall and little coal stoves in the classrooms. These were stoked in the morning and by the end of the day were out. My knees were permanently blue-red with cold above my long socks; my nose dripped. When I complained of the cold to Stella she laughed.

'Call this cold? Just you wait until winter has really started.' Then her eyes filled with sympathy. 'It must be harder for you, though, if you've never had to bear the cold in your life before.'

'I've got every bit of my winter uniform on and I'm still cold.'

'Try wearing all your vests at once. Three, even four. You're thin, you can take it. Ever had a chilblain?'

'No.'

'They're lovely fun, I can tell you.'

17

As the date of my parents' departure crept nearer we all became uneasy and restless. They'd been house hunting and had found nothing they particularly wanted to live in when they retired. Then about three weeks before they left, they went to see an old farmhouse which was due to be sold when its aged sick owner died. It was tucked away in a dip near the magnificent cliffs at Pleinmont.

My parents took me to see La Falaise, as the house was called, and since we couldn't go inside it that day they spent ages looking at the barns and greenhouses. I got bored and went off to find the cliff path. It was a grey foggy day and the Hanoi lighthouse gave its regular booming gun-like noise. Below me were savage rocks, clouded by mist. There was a German bunker, a look-out post staring blankly out to sea. I hadn't seen inside a bunker yet, so I followed the rabbit path to the rusting iron door. It screeched as I pulled it open and to my surprise I saw that someone was living there. There was a filthy old coat on a nail and a battered empty bucket by the door. A flight of steps led to a lower room and a smell of old cooking and humans and animals – like Jean the cowman's, strong but not too bad – wafted up them. Then I heard sounds behind me and quickly turned to leave.

As I stepped out of the door, a wild-looking man appeared followed by a goat. The man had a matted frizz of long greyish hair and a full beard which was equally matted. His boots were laced up with string and his khaki greatcoat was old and filthy. His eyes were dark, vague, a bit strange, but he smiled shyly at me. The goat gazed at me with its big yellow eyes bisected with a sharp black line of pupil. The two of them were faintly familiar and then I realized I had seen them cut off on Lihou Island.

'Sorry, I didn't mean to trespass.'

'It isn't private property,' said the man softly. 'Anyone can go in.'

'Isn't it your home?'

The man's eyes went blank. 'At the moment. I move about.'

'Do you like it out here on the cliffs?'

He stared out at the fog and seemed to have forgotten I was there. He was clearly a bit mad. As I was leaving, he said:

'I must be free. Free. Yet I've no choice. Come, Daphne.' Then he and the goat went into the bunker.

Mum and Dad were calling me by the time I got back to La Falaise. Mum's face was pink with excitement.

'Oh, Nancy, I'm so thrilled with this house! I wish we could have shown you the inside.'

'I like being near the cliffs.'

'So do I. I love that house, Bernard, I love it. We must buy it. And it's so cheap . . .'

'Only because nothing's been done to it since it was built two hundred years ago. It's going to take a lot of money to bring it into the twentieth century.'

'Do you know, Nancy, there's still the old furze

oven and old Mr Jehan actually used it during the war.'

'What's a furze oven?'

'Gorse was burned to cook with. The old lead pump in the kitchen's original, too, 1731 is stamped on it. And there's the most wonderful collection of oil lamps.'

'I suppose we make an offer for the contents too. Mr Jehan has no immediate family. The agent described the furniture as very old-fashioned and offered to have it cleared.'

'Bernard, we mustn't let him! That house is like a museum.'

'Some of that heavy Victorian stuff is hideous, of course.'

'I *like* it.' My parents argued and discussed happily all the way home and I thought about the old tramp. I'd got used to seeing beggars everywhere in India, I'd got used to extreme poverty. But this man was different, he wasn't like a beggar and though he was poor he didn't have the air of a real destitute. There was something about him that fascinated me; a stillness in his strange eyes. I wondered how he and his goat survived the cold winter living as they did.

18

'Talk some Indian.'

'No.'

'Go on, Nancy. You're such a spoil sport.' Betty Bougourd's square face was covered with freckles

136

and her eyes bulged out. Her lips were fat, as if they were about to burst out of their skin. She really was the ugliest girl I'd ever seen.

'Why should I?'

'Because none of us have ever heard Indian, that's why. Intellectual curiosity.' She gave a mocking hoot of laughter at her wit and made a quick grab for my pencil case which she waved about her head. The case had been given to me as a farewell present by my class at Pinemount School and it meant a lot to me.

'Give that back.'

Betty and her gang started throwing it from one to the other. 'Only if you talk some Indian.'

'There is no such thing as Indian,' I said through gritted teeth. 'There are over two hundred different languages in India, all with their own names.'

'Isn't that interesting, girls?' The pencil case flew about and I made a fruitless grab for it. 'Oh ho, aren't we getting cross?'

I stood stock still while Betty waved the case in front of my nose. I wanted to sink my teeth into her arm. Fury filled me.

'*Mut karo! Tum soor ka butcha!*' I shouted.

'Girls, girls, she's talking Indian at last!'

'Give me my case.'

'Come on, let's have some more, Nancy, that's not enough.'

'You're a pig, Betty, a real pig.' Stella's loud voice rode over the noise just as Miss Brackenbridge came in.

'Stella, not only are you always talking, but you're being offensive while you do it.'

'But Miss Brackenbridge—'

'I'm tired of your excuses. I'm going to give you a detention. Silence, everybody.'

Betty handed me back the pencil case at once and was now sitting looking bland. I was still shaking with rage, but I was comforted that Stella had taken my side, and the fact that she, like me, had coincidentally called Betty the same thing. I'd called her the offspring of a pig, in India the most serious insult for a race that finds the pig unclean.

Stella came and walked with me when we set off soon after towards the games pitch, half a mile away, for a hockey lesson.

'Betty Bougourd's father drives a scent wagon.'

'Sorry?'

'Scent wagon . . . sewage lorry. They come and empty out our cesspools. Great black tubes suck it all into the lorry.'

'I've never seen one.'

'You will. Country folk aren't on main drains.'

I thought about Happy, our Untouchable sweeper, and his awful job of emptying the thunderboxes.

'It can't be a very pleasant job, driving a sewage lorry.'

'Horrible. Betty keeps very quiet about it, she's ashamed and I don't blame her. I don't think anyone knows except me and now you.' We could hear Betty's raucous voice not far behind us in the crocodile of girls.

'It must be dreadful to be ashamed of what your father does—' I stopped, because Betty and Ann de Garis had moved up and were now just behind us. Stella and I tried to ignore them; Betty obviously hadn't done with baiting me. Then, just as we reached the gates of the games pitch, she was overcome with a fit of sneezing . . . huge juicy sneezes. Calmly, she reached out and blew her nose on the end of my school scarf.

Something went snap inside me. I swung my games bag full of heavy studded hockey boots and brought it down on Betty's head as hard as I could. Her knees buckled and she passed out.

'We want to hear exactly what happened from *you*. The official version wasn't very pleasant.' My father and mother were gazing sternly at me; we were sitting in the parlour, cold with its fire unlit. They had been rung up by Miss Porrit who told them she was sending me home to cool down as I was a menace to the other girls. 'She also said she was considering expelling you, or at least suspending you. I feel she is overreacting, but I want the facts before I go in and sort all this out.'

So I told them every detail, all except the conversation with Stella about Betty's father. A part of me was uneasy about Betty, while most of me hated her. And I couldn't help feeling a sense of triumph when I knocked her out.

'Right. The girl's a bully, but you shouldn't have hit her. Nancy, write a letter of apology to this Betty Bougourd and I will take it in myself now and talk to Miss Porrit. This has to be cleared up before we leave Guernsey.'

So my father went to St Peter Port in Aunt Sophie's Baby Austin and charmed Miss Porrit while I helped Mum sort and pack their things. The knocking-out of Betty happened on a Friday and my parents were leaving on the following Monday.

Dad returned with good news; I could go in as normal on Monday, but on probation.

'Miss Porrit said if anything else of a violent nature happened, she would expel you.' My father and I smiled at each other; I'd never been violent before, I wasn't a violent person. 'Betty Bougourd sent you this.'

Betty had written a note on a piece of file paper; she had returned to the classroom at lunchtime, no more than bruised.

'Sorry I messed your scarf. It was not a nice thing to do. B. Bougourd.'

19

That Sunday my grandparents gave a great family tea. Even though I'd been in Guernsey long enough to get used to a vast extended family, it was still a shock to see quite so many relatives in one house. Great aunts and great uncles, aunts and uncles, cousins I hadn't met before screaming and yelling with excitement as they played a game in the basement. I decided the best thing to do was help Grand-mère in the kitchen because then I had somewhere legitimate to escape to.

'What a helpful person we are,' said Great Aunt Letty. 'You must come to tea with us on your own soon. Then you could see my collection properly.' She put her frightening face close to mine.

'And the cats,' whispered Great Aunt Susannah with a sly smile. Grand-mère shooed them out of the kitchen.

'Butter these scones while they're hot, Nancy. There.' She put a pat of bright yellow Guernsey butter on the table. 'Use that for a treat. Does Sophie still make butter?'

'I don't think so.'

'Too busy I suppose. Sophie's always been too busy for frills, mind you. Robert's orchids drove her mad.' My grandmother split scones for me to spread. 'Orchids. Useless flowers, she always said. He used to spend hours in the greenhouse tending the wretched things while she exhausted herself working the farm. They all died anyway, that first winter of the Occupation. How are you getting on at the College?'

'All right.' I saw Betty sinking slowly to her knees . . .

'I'm surprised. I never liked that headmistress. Joyless woman. She looks very like my Grandmother Heaume, though I know there's no connection. I didn't like that grandmother either. She had a beard—'

'A beard?'

'Well, so much hair on her chin that it looked like a beard to me. I was about your age when I was taken to see her on her death-bed. She was in a four-poster bed, with a mob-cap on and her beard showed up against her white skin. She didn't open her eyes until she suddenly said to my aunt who looked after her and was fussing round the bed: "*Ferme ta goule et soins tes poules, Adele.*" She died next day.'

'What did that mean?'

'Shut up and go and look after your chickens.' Her eyes glinted as I laughed. 'I was supposed to look like that grandmother. I used to have night-mares in case I grew a beard too.'

I was just about to say I felt the same when people said I looked like Great Aunt Letty, when Mum came in with a grizzling Clare on her hip and gave her a scone to eat.

'You spoil that child,' said Grand-mère. The atmosphere in the kitchen changed at once; my grandmother frowned and re-arranged the plates of food, my mother sighed and stared out of the window without replying. Clare chewed messily at the scone. Then into the tension came gloomy Uncle John and stood beside Mum. It was impossible to believe they were related, let alone brother and sister.

'I hear you're buying La Falaise,' he said.

'Yes.' Mum didn't look at him.

'Old Mr Jehan could live for years.'

'We're in no hurry. Anyway he's agreed to sell it to us and accepted a deposit.'

'It'll be empty a long time.'

'Sophie's going to keep an eye on it.'

'I could pop in now and again for you.'

I could see Mum was trying to refuse without hurting him. Clare created a diversion by dropping her half-eaten scone on the floor.

'There's a lot of good stuff in that house, they tell me. It might get stolen.'

'All the valuables are in the bank. There's noth-ing there that would interest a thief.' Mum's tone was sharp.

'So you don't want me to keep an eye on it?'

'Sophie can manage, thanks. It's near her. You're in the Vale. Too far.' Mum's voice was taking on a

Guernsey lilt from her brother's very strong accent.

'John, take these scones into the dining-room would you? Don't eat them on the way,' said his mother crisply.

'No-one trusts me,' he said and went out.

'One's children never change,' said Grand-mère.

'Well, you'll be free of me from tomorrow.'

Grand-mère looked at Mum and opened her arms. They clung together, saying nothing, for a long time, while I held sticky Clare.

20

'The photographer's come!'

Somehow Abraham and Esmée Queripel managed to seat their family – all thirty-five – in the end of their large drawing-room. I was in a row on the floor with Clare on my lap, next to Marie and Pierre and some of Great Uncle Basil's grandchildren. The photographer fiddled about, disappearing under his black cloth and moving his tripod a quarter of an inch this way and half an inch that way. Clare and the other babies kept wriggling and escaping. The noise was immense.

'Hush!' shouted Grand-père. 'How can poor Mr Grut concentrate!'

Then two children had to go to the lavatory. Eventually Mr Grut and the Queripel tribe were ready simultaneously and we were told to say cheese and keep still. The shutter moved with a satisfying click. Mr Grut managed to take three photographs before the front line broke ranks again.

Then we all stood up and I saw Aunt Sophie had tears in her eyes.

'The whole family's together, except for Abraham who's dead and Robert who's missing,' whispered Dad. 'That's why she's crying.'

'Are we going home soon?'

'Now, if I have my way . . .' He winked at me.

'Grand-mère. This is broken, did you know?' Pierre stood holding the tin tiger I had found in the cellar. 'It was working last time we were here.'

'Oh, Helen, do you remember that tiger? You sent it to Abraham years ago.' My grandmother took the tiger and held it up. 'We called him Tippoo.'

'It's broken,' repeated Pierre. 'I'm really sad. I loved that tiger.' I hid myself behind a mass of bodies. I wanted to confess I'd done it, but my tongue felt as if it was glued to my mouth. Grand-mère tried to wind the key. It made a thin rasping noise.

'Oh dear. Well, it's been well-used and well-loved. These things don't last for ever.' And she put it high on the mantelpiece. The tiger glared down in my direction, its teeth bared.

21

The taxi smelled of leather and sick. Dad and I and the luggage were in it, as we had been on my first journey through Guernsey. Mum and Clare followed in the Baby Austin, miles behind. Dad took out a pound note and folded it into my hand.

'This is an extra from me to you. I've already arranged with Sophie that she'll give you your pocket-money, a shilling a week, the same as the twins, but I wanted you to have a nest-egg, in case you need something in an emergency.'

It was a lovely crisp new Guernsey note and I sniffed it before I put it into the inside pocket of my school blazer. Dad took my hand and held it tight.

'I'm glad we're on our own. I can't help admitting I worry about leaving you behind, even though there's nothing to be done about it. I think you could be quite unhappy, chicken, but then you expect that. Sophie and her family can't help being affected by Robert's disappearance . . . in fact, they'd all feel a lot better if they knew finally that he was dead. Then they could mourn him and get over it. And they may hear news while you're there . . . it could be difficult for you.'

'Do you think he's dead?'

'Yes, I do. Otherwise he would have been found by now. But either way you'll be living with a family with a heavy heart. I wish you could have boarded somewhere else, but Helen and Sophie have always been so close it wasn't even considered. I suggested your grandparents, but your mother felt they were too old to cope with a young person permanently in the house.'

'It would have been more convenient for school.'

My father looked sharply at me. 'Don't even entertain the idea, Nancy. Helen says it would upset Sophie to have you moved.'

'There's more to do and more company at Maison de Haut, I suppose.' But I thought of my comfortable conversation the day before with my grandmother.

'Exactly. I know you'll cope because you're resilient and don't give in easily. But I really do understand how difficult it could be. Don't forget that.' He squeezed my hand. I wanted to cry, but I stopped myself. 'Keep busy, Nancy, that's the great thing. Don't brood about India. Keep busy. Join clubs at school, get a good group of friends round you. Have you made any real friends at the college yet?'

'The girl I like has another best friend.'

'It's early days. She might come to realize you're more her type . . . give her time.'

We drove along in silence for a while, then I said: 'You won't forget to give Bruce my present when you see him, will you?'

'Of course not. I should think the Allotsons will be the first people we'll see. We'll go to the Horseshoe Falls together and think of our Nancy. And we'll send you photographs of the new house as soon as it's finished . . . Ian said in his last letter that the work is progressing fast.'

I let my father talk on; my heart felt so full I didn't trust myself to speak without breaking down. Soon the harbour was in front of us, screeching cranes, rattling chains, crying gulls. The mail-boat was already in from Jersey on its way to Weymouth. A small black car was being swung precariously over the ship; it looked very odd as it went nose downwards into the hold.

'Oh dear.'

'What is it, Dad?'

'Look.'

A large group of Queripels were waiting to see my parents off. Fury banished my pain; I'd expected to have this last half an hour alone with them and Clare, except for Aunt Sophie, and there ahead of me were my grandparents, the Little Aunts, Great Uncle Basil and, worst of all, Uncle John. They were all beaming.

'Thought we'd give you a little surprise,' said Great Aunt Letty. 'Give you a royal send-off.'

I wanted to scream, 'Go away all of you, go away.' I wanted to push them all into the harbour. I hate goodbyes at the best of times and this was the worst.

'How kind,' said my father flatly. A porter came up to help with the luggage and from that point on there wasn't a moment's peace. There were people everywhere, my parents were rushing about distracted, the harbour noises were deafening. For some time I sat on a crate with Clare on my lap, until dockers came and said they had to load it. So Clare and I went to stare at the little boats in the harbour, but she was upset by all the activity around and kept agitating for Mum whom I couldn't see anywhere. Then the mail-boat let off a couple of warning blasts from its siren and Mum came running towards us. Suddenly I was hugging my mother for the last time in two years.

'Can't I come on board for a bit?'

'They're sending visitors off now, she's about to sail. Oh Nancy . . .' Her eyes were full of tears. I didn't feel like crying any more, I was so numb. I watched my parents stumble up the gangway and in no time the mail-boat was creeping slowly backwards out of the harbour, its siren honking to warn small boats of its progress. That noise of a ship's siren brought back the steamers on the wide brown Brahmaputra and the sound rang and rang in my ears as my family disappeared out of sight through the grey granite walls of the harbour mouth.

22

Aunt Sophie dropped me off at the College on her way home. As I was getting out she said:

'You don't have to go to school today if you can't stand it.' She did not meet my eye, but her voice was softer than usual. I hesitated; I thought of the cold stoniness of Maison de Haut, of the silence with just Aunt Sophie at home. School would at least be warmer and take my mind off my parents and Clare sailing across the Channel.

'It's OK, I'll go to school.' I watched the Baby Austin labour on up the hill and then turned into the drive. The College buildings ahead of me were in the usual grey granite, the drive and the playground were of dark grey asphalt. Cold grey hardness was entering my body, my mind, my soul. I began to feel as if I was in my own nightmare.

The grey playground stretched ahead of me like a flattened sea that was about to start rising and undulating. Waves, waves, they were rippling towards me—

'Are you all right, Nancy?' Miss Keddy, the domestic science teacher, had come out of the classroom adjacent to the playground. She put a hand on my shoulder. 'You look very white.

Come and sit down.' She led me to a bench.

'I feel giddy.'

'I'll get you a drink of water.' She came back with a cup of cold water which I sipped. 'It'll be break soon. Do you want to stay here in the playground or go to the sickroom?'

'I'll go to my classroom.' I stood up, in a hurry to leave the playground before hordes of children poured into it. 'Thanks, Miss Keddy.'

'I should go to the sickroom and lie down for a bit, if I were you. You still look very white.'

I went into the cloakroom to hang my coat up, wishing with all my heart that I'd gone home with Aunt Sophie. I stood stock still by my peg, unable to move.

'Hi there, Nancy. You're late today.' It was Stella. 'Hey, what's the matter?'

'I don't feel very well.'

'Nor do I. Miss Brackenbridge has just told me to lie down in the sickroom for a bit.'

'Miss Keddy has just told me to do the same.'

Stella grinned. 'Why are we waiting? Come on, quick, before the break bell rings.'

The sickroom was beyond all the offices, the secretary's, the bursar's and the caretaker's. No-one saw us go in. Since there was only one bed, we sat on it with our backs to the wall. Stella got an apple out of her pocket and broke it in half by twisting it between her hands.

'That's clever.'

'Dead easy, if you know how.'

'Show me. I've got an apple as well.' I took it out of my satchel and she showed me exactly what to do.

'Put your thumbs here, near the stem. Twist while pulling the apple apart. Go on, hard.'

With a satisfying crack, the red and yellow apple split open into two well-balanced halves.

'What a neat trick.' Pleased with ourselves, we crunched our apples.

'Did you have apples in India?'

'Big red ones, used to come from Kashmir, up in the Himalayas on the other side of India from us. But they were a treat, we didn't have them often. The fruit I ate all the time was bananas and oranges and papayas.'

'Papayas?' I explained what a papaya was like until I could almost taste the rich sweet yellow flesh. 'What's the thing you miss most about India?'

'My horse and the rides we did in the early mornings.'

'You could have a horse here.'

'It wouldn't be the same. Besides, it was cheap there. We couldn't afford to have a horse in Guernsey.'

'I've never ridden a horse and I'm not likely to. Can't afford the lessons let alone the horse. Dad's broke all the time.'

'What does he do?'

'Grows tomatoes. But he's known as Bill the Blight because his plants are always dying.' Stella finished her apple, core and all. 'Mind you, I'm not surprised. He spends all his time with his pigeons. Drives Mum mad. She's called Cherry and she works down at the Odeon cinema. She called me Stella because she'd heard it meant star in Latin and she thought that might help me be a star myself one day. Really. I think she was serious.'

'My parents are called Bernard and Helen.' A wave of pain overcame me and I put my forehead on my bent knees. 'They left for India this morning. They'll be gone for two years.'

'Oh God, Nancy. No wonder you feel awful. Two years. Who are you living with while they're away?'

'My Aunt Sophie Le Patourel in St Peters.'

'But two years. It's a lifetime. You'll be like strangers when they get back.'

'My little sister won't even recognize me.' I thought of Clare's warm pudgy body and missed her achingly.

'Is your aunt strict?'

'She's a bit of a dragon.'

'You must come and stay with me one week-end. My parents are so dreamy they haven't a clue what's going on. I climb out of my bedroom window and they don't even know I've gone out. Come and stay, Nancy and we'll have some fun. They have a good social on Saturdays down at the church hall. Do you like dancing?'

'I've never learned. I'm supposed to be starting lessons soon.'

Stella leapt up. 'I'll teach you, I'm a real whizz at dancing! Quickstep, Waltz, Foxtrot, Tango . . . I'm brilliant at them all though I say so myself!' She laughed and pulled me to my feet. 'Come on, Nancy, let's start with a waltz. Now, you count one, two, three, one, two, three and watch my feet. La la di di dah, di dah, di dah, la la di di dah, di dah, di dah . . .'

In our Clarks' crêpe-soled sandals we started to shuffle round the green linoleum floor. We didn't get far. The door swung open and there was Miss Porrit.

'What is going on?' she thundered. 'This is a sickroom, not a dancing studio.'

'We're both sick,' began Stella.

'I will not have impertinence. Go and wait outside my study, Stella Marquand.'

'But Miss Brackenbridge will tell you that she sent me to lie down—'

'*Go!*' Stella went. 'Now, Nancy, perhaps you'll tell me what you're doing in the sickroom? I should have thought after your exploits of last week you'd take very great care not to get into trouble. I suppose you're going to tell me that Miss Brackenbridge sent you here too.'

'Miss Keddy did. She saw me in the playground—' I stopped.

'Yes?' I couldn't go on. The expanse of grey heaving asphalt filled my brain again, like the sea that was bearing my family away from me by the minute. 'Go on, Nancy. Surely Miss Keddy didn't send you to the sickroom just for standing in the playground.' Miss Porrit's voice was solid sarcasm.

Then it was as if everything became unlocked inside me. I burst into tears; my sobs seemed to have been waiting just below the surface. They knocked me over with their violence so that I collapsed face down on the sickroom bed.

'Nancy! What is all this about? Take a grip on yourself! Goodness me!' Miss Porrit was beginning to bleat. I was beyond saying anything. 'This is ridiculous. I'll return when you've composed yourself. I was on my way to the bursar when I heard the sound of someone singing the "Blue Danube"

. . . I haven't got the time to waste on you girls . . .'
She went out still talking.

I had a really good cry; I let the pain and
frustration and sense of loss pour out. I didn't want
to be in Guernsey. I didn't want to be at the College.
I didn't want the life that had been wished on me
for the next two years. All I wanted was to be with
my parents and Clare in the lovely corner of Assam
where my life had begun.

As I sobbed my brain filled with a succession of
images of waterfalls and pine-trees and Why Not
and Bahyong and Fuss and Congreeal and Laughing and Rinjo. I didn't hear the door open and close,
didn't feel anyone sit down beside me. Slowly the
sobs left me, the whirl of images faded and as I
continued to lie face down on the edge of exhausted
sleep a voice said:

'Nancy. I brought you a drink of orange juice.'
Stella was sitting beside me, quiet and relaxed. She
held a glass of well-diluted squash. I sat up and
sipped it.

'What is Miss Porrit going to do?'

'Nothing. She sent you this orange herself.
Underneath that corset beats a human heart.' Stella
grinned at me, a litle ruefully. 'When I told her why
you were upset, she became almost human to prove
it. She didn't forget to give me a detention for
waltzing in school, but she did tell me to come and
sit with you until you felt better, so she can't be all
that bad.'

I became aware that the school was full of noise;
break was ending with a crashing of feet along
corridors and up stairs.

'How are you feeling, Nancy? Still sick?'

'Much better.' I finished the orange. 'What about you? You were feeling sick too, after all.'

'Dancing makes me feel better.' Stella gave her gurgly laugh. 'Even if it didn't last long. La la di di dah, di dah, di dah,' she hummed, grinning.

'Will you teach me another time?'

'Of course I will.'

We heard heavy footsteps coming to the sick-room door and Miss Porrit's face came round it.

'Ah, looking better I see, Nancy.'

'Thanks for the drink of orange.'

'I'll take my glass back then. Well, are you two ready to rejoin the class?'

'Yes, Miss Porrit.'

'In that case off you go.'

'Yes, Miss Porrit.' When we got out of earshot, Stella said in an excellent imitation of Miss Porrit's voice: 'And please, Nancy, try not to knock out any more classmates.'

23

Both Stella and I had our first periods that night. Stella's happened half way through the evening and since neither she nor her mother had made any preparations, she had to make do with her mother's stuff.

Mum had given me a little cardboard box before she left. 'You're bound to need this before I next see you.' My period started in the middle of the night and as I reached for the box I blessed her for her forethought. Inside the box was a pink elastic belt with pink metal hooks and two packets of Dr White's sanitary towels which she'd wrapped in pink tissue paper so thin that the writing showed through. There was also a tin of Cusson's Apple Blossom Talc which smelled delicious when I sprinkled it liberally over myself. I pushed my soiled pyjamas under the bed to deal with later – Marie's dirty socks were still there – and lay down again. The pad was uncomfortable and the belt a bit tight; I loosened it and lay there, sleep far away. I thought of my womb; I imagined a little bag like a balloon filled with red ink. My breasts itched, but that was nothing new. I lay there and watched the black ceiling turn into dark beams with lighter boards above. A cock crowed in the yard; other cocks answered him; dogs barked in return. Then footsteps crunched quietly up the lane, accompanied by a pattering noise. Curious to see who was up so early, I went to my window.

There walking past slowly was the old tramp and his goat. He looked up at the house and caught sight of me behind my closed window. Down went his head and on he hurried; the goat took some bites off a bush near the gate and then hurried after his master.

What a strange life he must lead, wandering about outside everyone else's lives. He'd had a bag on his back; he probably went out early so that he could steal from fields and orchards at first light. He'd no doubt had his eye on Aunt Sophie's apples. I was sorry I'd put him off. There were so many windfalls, he was welcome. Perhaps I'd drop some round to him when I biked over to keep an eye on La Falaise as I'd promised my parents I'd do.

My parents . . . I was sure that by timing my first period like this my body was saying grow up, grow up. I decided I wanted to keep it a secret from Aunt Sophie for the moment. I had enough money to buy my own pads every month.

Every month. Every month for years and years and years and years . . . unthinkable time stretched away in front of me, time almost as frightening as death. Cold with terror, I jumped back into bed and pulled the covers over my head. But this was no help; I felt as if I'd suddenly woken up to find myself trapped on a moving escalator, like the long wooden ones that had so fascinated me in the London Underground. Only this escalator had no visible end and there was no way I could escape from it.

Maison de Haut was horribly silent at breakfast. Usually Clare was banging her spoon and making her noises and Mum and Sophie were chattering while the other Le Patourels ate in silence and then disappeared to work or school.

'Porridge?' Aunt Sophie had already dolloped a sticky portion for me. I still hated porridge, but if I just had bread and jam – my butter ration had run out – I got so hungry later. Bacon and eggs were for week-ends.

No-one said good-morning in the Le Patourel household, or gave much sign they'd seen me come in. Basil was just finishing, Marie and Pierre were their impenetrable selves.

'Are you feeling all right?' asked Aunt Sophie, frowning.

'I didn't sleep very well.' Silence descended again. I finished my lumpy porridge and didn't have time to toast my bread. I was just getting my coat and beret on in the dark cold hall with its one small window, when Aunt Sophie appeared.

'Are you really all right? Don't go to school if you're not feeling up to it.'

'I'm fine.' The pads between my legs felt fat and unwieldy. There was a pause as I wound my scarf round my neck. Then to my surprise she came over and hugged me.

'I'm going to miss them too. Miss them dreadfully, particularly Helen. So I do understand, Nancy, I do understand. Please feel you can talk freely to me.'

'Yes, Aunt Sophie.' We smiled at each other, but both of us knew that though the gulf between us had narrowed in that moment, it was still a gulf.

'Go out of the front door. It's quicker.'

'But it's always locked.'

'Time we stopped that. It's just laziness.' My aunt struggled with the old bolts and the door eventually swung open, creaking loudly. She stood and watched me go down the short path to the lane. When I turned to wave goodbye before I went out of sight round a corner, she was still there.

24

'Hullo.'

The tramp stared at me in silence. His goat was cropping the short cliff grass nearby.

'Would you like some windfalls?'

'Windfalls?' He said the word as if he didn't understand it.

'Apples. Look. Have them, give them to your goat if you don't need them.'

'Thank you.' He was sitting on an outcrop of granite on the cliff, nearer La Falaise than his bunker. His eyes were red, so was his nose; he looked as if he had a cold. 'What's your name?' He followed this with a dreadful coughing fit.

'Nancy.'

'That's a yankee name.'

'I don't know where it comes from.'

'It's yankee. My goat's name is Greek. Daphne. What a beautiful sound that has, don't you agree? Daphne.'

'Yes. She's a beautiful goat.'

But he shut his red-rimmed eyes and went off into a dream. I stood there for a bit, watching Daphne and then decided to go. As I moved away, he opened his eyes again.

'Have you got an aspirin, by any chance?'

'Sorry. Do you need one badly?'

'An aspirin would help.'

I stared at him feeling useless. I had no money with me, I didn't know where the nearest chemist was either. But I could fetch him some aspirins from Maison de Haut.

'If you like, I'll go and get you some. How many would you like?'

He had another coughing fit even worse than the last and then sat there exhausted, swaying slightly, his eyes closed.

'I'll be back as soon as I can with your aspirins.'

The chain came off my bike on the way up L'Eree

158

hill; my fingers got pinched and covered with oil as I put it back on. When I finally got home Aunt Sophie wanted me to help her hang some curtains. By the time I'd cleaned my hands, helped her and taken some aspirins from a big jar in the medicine cupboard, well over an hour had passed. I rushed back to the cliff near La Falaise, but there was no sign of the tramp or his goat. I went to his bunker and called 'hullo' a few times, but no-one came. The wind blew strongly off the rough sea; it was cold and salty and my eyes watered. I looked along the cliff to see if the tramp was somewhere down there. Except for the seagulls, there wasn't a soul around.

I turned his old bucket upside down and put the screw of paper containing the aspirins on it. Spatters of rain fell; there was a big black cloud coming in fast from the Atlantic. It reached me halfway home; not only was I then soaked through, but the chain came off my bike again just as the rain grew heavy.

'Nancy! I've been looking for you everywhere. Your parents have this minute rung up. They wanted to have a final chat before they boarded the ship. I simply couldn't find you anywhere.'

'Are they ringing back?' Rain dripped off me as I stared at her.

'They couldn't . . . they were literally on the point of boarding.' I wanted to weep with frustration. 'They didn't say much, just wanted to communicate. Oh, Helen said to tell you that Clare keeps saying Nancy all the time. It's her first proper word.'

Clare. I thought of her small person as she bustled about, legs working hard under the bulge of her nappy. My little sister Clare. I could see Mum,

Dad and Clare on the deck watching England recede . . . I went to the sink to wash the oil off my hands while my pain built up inside me. Then I went upstairs, but not to cry. I felt too frustrated to cry. Just because of that stupid tramp I'd missed talking to my parents and hearing Clare say 'Nancy, Nancy' down the 'phone. The ship would sail past the Channel Islands and my family would hold me in their minds as I would hold them. I thought of the smells on board a liner: rope, new paint, sea-water, scrubbed decks, food smells from the galleys and alcohol smells from the bars. I knew they would be sitting down to eat soon, at the same time as us, but instead of the kitchen table at Maison de Haut they would be in the restaurant with its starched white table-cloths and shiny cutlery and printed menus in holders. Even welsh rarebit and scrambled eggs looked special when typed out on a menu . . .

I lay on my bed and stared blankly at the ceiling. Darkness fell but I didn't switch the light on. I was utterly miserable.

25

'Nancy! Come to Herm! Dad's taking out my uncle's boat to go fishing today and he says he'll put us down on Herm for a couple of hours. We'll take a picnic.' Stella's lively voice and the calm fine day after the storm immediately banished my gloom. I met the Marquands in St Peter Port, on the Castle Cornet pier. Stella ran to meet me.

'I'm so glad you could come . . . and it's a perfect day. I love Herm in the winter.'

'I've never been.'

The little island of Herm was a few miles off, between Guernsey and Sark. We gazed across at its small shape in delighted anticipation all the way across the gently-swelling sea. Bill Marquand, a vague-looking man with a wild woolly look, stood whistling at the helm; Cherry, who was small and thin with red permed hair, chatted in the tiny cabin to a friend. Stella and I sat, well wrapped up, on the narrow section of deck beyond the cabin at the prow.

'We'll walk all round the island . . . it's so small it only takes about an hour. But what I can't wait to do is search the Shell Beach. Nobody collected any shells throughout the war so it's absolutely full of them.'

We were dropped at the small harbour and told to be back there in two hours' time without fail.

'Don't leave it longer, or the tide will be too low.'

'Good fishing, Dad.'

Stella's mother stuck her head out of the cabin. 'None of your tricks, Stella Marquand. We'll leave you behind if you do what you did last time.'

Stella and I set off at a brisk pace along the narrow unmade road. There were a few old houses and cottages, most of them shut up for the winter. I loved Herm the moment I set foot on it. I loved the sharp rise of cliff at one end, sloping quickly to the flat area of common at the other. Herm was shaped exactly like a fish, with the common at the tail end.

'Last time we came Marion and I forgot how late it was, we were so busy looking for shells. My

161

parents were late getting the boat back and my uncle wasn't pleased.'

I hoped Marion wouldn't hear that I had taken her place on the boat. She was the sort of person to be upset by that. She'd been giving me black looks recently as it was.

But Herm was so beautiful I pushed everything else out of my mind. Little tracks overhung with trees, snugly-sited cottages, coves and rocks at the high end; long sandy beaches interrupted by clumps of rock all round the low part. And in the lea of every clump of rocks there was a magic heap of shells, lying in order as if sorted into sizes by the tide. Oh those shells! Five years of war had brought so many that all the visitors since the war ended hadn't made much impression on them. Stella and I picked up dozens, exclaiming endlessly in delight. I loved the simple cowrie shell: I found one that was three inches long, the longest Stella said she'd ever seen. It was a deep blush pink with freckles; within its ridged mouth I could hear the hushing noise of deep oceans.

'Cowries bring good luck. And that one is amazing, really amazing.'

'I'll see if I can find another one for you.' But for all my searching, the cowrie remained unique. I was sure that another must be lurking somewhere, but if it was, it eluded me.

'Let's have a quick look at the 'plane before we go.'

For there, wrecked in the middle of Mouison-nière beach, was a heap of twisted grey metal. A British 'plane had been shot down; Stella didn't know if the pilot had survived. Most of the 'plane had been taken away for souvenirs by the locals, but we found a small straight piece which I decided to take back with me.

'If you bend the edges, you could make it into an ashtray . . . I made one like that. Come on, Nancy, we ought to go, we'll have to run as it is. It always takes longer than you expect to get back to the harbour.'

As we puffed along, our rucksacks empty of picnic but heavy with shells, I realized I'd hardly given my family a thought all day long. Across the Little Russel was Guernsey, so hated yesterday, so comfortless. Greenhouses glinted in the afternoon sun. It looked very benign today.

When I got home I would put my beautiful cowries, large and small, into Bruce's elephant box.

26

'Who is it?' Grand-père peered across the front garden, secateurs in hand.

'Nancy.'

'Of course . . . I didn't recognize you in your school uniform and your green beret. Come in, come in. Let's go and find Esmée.' He led me into the house, walking earth into the hall.

Grand-mère was sitting in the drawing-room curled up in a huge tattered chair, reading. Her half-moon glasses were right on the end of her nose.

'Who is it?'

'Nancy,' I said again.

'Nancy, what a lovely surprise! Come and give

me a kiss before I haul myself to my feet. I'm getting so stiff.' So I kissed her and sat on a footstool beside her when she showed no signs of actually moving. She took my beret off. 'Nancy, all in her green uniform.'

'I hate bottle green.'

'I hate it too. Pale green, leaf green, apple green, sea green, emerald green, are all lovely,' she said dreamily, 'but bottle green is hard and dull. And it doesn't suit you, which is rather unfair as you have to wear it all the time.'

I leaned back against her chair, feeling very at home. Grand-père had already pottered back to the garden.

'Tell me what you've been up to since your parents left. I suddenly realized this morning that it's exactly three weeks today they sailed out of the harbour. Time does fly.'

Not for me; each day had made its long hours felt, except for the lovely time with Stella in Herm.

'Nothing much except school.'

'Come and help me make a cup of tea while we talk.' She took her half-moons off and used my shoulder to lever herself up. She patted my hair. 'Nice hair, Sykes hair. The Queripels don't have lovely curly hair like that.' I followed her into the kitchen, hoping she wouldn't ask me why I'd dropped in. I'd come because I couldn't help myself; somehow when I left school I couldn't go straight to the bus-stop. I'd seen Marion Evans invite Stella to walk down to the town, so I didn't want to follow them. Without a conscious decision I had found myself wandering towards my grandparents' house above St Peter Port.

Grand-mère made tea and toast and the three of us sat there very cosily beside the old black range. Then a spatter of rain hit the window and I realized it was nearly dark outside.

'I ought to go. Perhaps I should ring Aunt Sophie and tell her where I am.'

Grand-père stood in the open kitchen door and looked out for a minute. 'There's a huge bank of black cloud coming over, it's going to rain cats and dogs in a minute.' As he spoke, another spatter of rain hit the window panes.

'You could spend the night here with us if you wanted, Nancy. You're going to get soaked otherwise.' Grand-mère spoke gruffly and began to clear away the tea things.

'I ought to go back . . .' I hesitated, wondering whether I'd got everything I needed for school the next day with me. Outside there was a flash of lightning followed quickly by thunder.

'You stay, my girl, no question. I'll go and telephone Sophie.'

'I'll do it,' said Grand-père. 'I wanted to talk to her anyway about her application for a widow's pension.'

'She won't apply, Aby. She says give it another year. She won't give up hope, that girl.'

I sat at the kitchen table helping my grandmother chop vegetables for a soup for supper and thinking how odd it was that to them my stern, sad Aunt Sophie was 'that girl.'

> *Rouge bonnet, veur-tu du lait?*
> *Nennin, ma mère, il est trop fre*
> *Rouge bonnet, veur-tu de la creme?*

Grand-mère sang as she and I made up my bed.

'I don't know what made me think of that one; I suppose it's because you're around. I used to sing it to all my children when they were little.'

'What does the patois mean?'

'Red bonnet – perhaps the child is wearing a red hat – do you want some milk? No, mother, it's too fresh. Red bonnet, do you want some cream? Yes, mother, that's what I love. It doesn't mean very much, but I don't think children like things with too much meaning, do you?'

'All children like songs about food,' I said with some surprise because I'd just realized it. 'My ayah used to sing us several like that. One was about bread butter and sugar, *roti, makhan, cini.*'

'Sing it to me.' Grand-mère sat down on the bed and patted it for me to join jer. I sang her *nini, baba, nini* imitating Congreeal's very nasal way of singing.

'Was she a nice ayah?'

'Congreeal was the most important person in my life after Mum and Dad.' Sometimes she had been the best person of all, but I didn't say that.

'So you miss her.'

'Yes, I do. By the time we left she was Clare's ayah really and my good friend. I wonder if she misses me, or thinks about me as much as I think of her?'

'She probably misses you more. The person who leaves a place often suffers less than the people who are left behind. You have got all the stimulus of a new life and they haven't.'

166

This was a novel idea to me and I considered it while we sat peacefully on the bed – Grand-mère never seemed in a hurry to go off and do something else, like most adults I knew.

'But I didn't want my new life. I wanted to go back to India with my parents and only leave it when they retired.'

'Helen left me with the impression that you were happy to stay behind in Guernsey.'

'I was desperate to go back to Assam.'

'You poor little thing.'

But I didn't like my grandmother calling me a poor little thing. She had been treating me like a friend up until then, not a child.

'I don't mind now. I'm managing.'

'I'm sure you are. You're a Guernesaise after all and all Guernsey people are tough. Tough, obstinate and sometimes crafty. That's us.' She got up and drew the long red and yellow striped curtains to shut out the beating rain. 'Now I'll leave you to do your homework until supper.'

The room was big and very high and full of huge furniture: an ornately carved wardrobe, a chest of drawers so tall that I could not see into the top drawers. There was a picture of a ship on a rough curling sea on one wall and above the bed was a sampler.

Mary Louisa Queripel, aged fourteen in the year of our Lord 1847, it said across the bottom. Above her name was a picture of Adam and Eve each side of a strangely-shaped green tree with a snake poking its head out of the ball of leaves at the top of the trunk. Eve was holding a large squarish apple and both she and Adam were wearing rather curious bathing suits instead of fig-leaves. Mary Louisa had added a row of sweet rabbits along the bottom of the sampler, jumping from left to right under her name. My ancestress had been my age when she'd done this large sampler, working with tiny stitches on fine linen.

Rebuked by her industry, I started on my homework.

Four clocks chimed every hour: a grandfather clock in the hall, a carriage clock in the drawing-room, a black marble clock in the dining-room and a round wall clock in the kitchen. All the doors were open when seven struck and the clocks seemed to race each other to finish first. I was hungry; we usually ate at six at Maison de Haut and I hadn't expected my grandparents to be different. I went downstairs cautiously; the house was silent except for the various ticking clocks.

There was no-one in the kitchen, though the vegetable soup was bubbling on the range. I peered into the drawing-room: empty. I found my grandparents in the dining-room, poring over a huge jigsaw which they'd obviously recently laid out on the table.

'No, no, Esmée, that bit of edge isn't sky.'

'Why not? It's blue.'

'There's a little pond in that corner, look, I'm sure that's where it belongs.'

'The pond's grey, not blue.'

'Ah, Nancy, come in and help us with your sharp young eyes.'

Ravenous, I began to search for pieces of edge energetically when Grand-père announced we'd have supper when we'd done all four edges. The clocks were all having a busy time striking the half hour as I found the last remaining piece of edge.

'Goodness, it's late. We're shockers when we've got a new jigsaw,' said Grand-mère. 'We forget the time completely.'

'There, I've done the rest of the pond.'

'You and your pond.'

At last we sat down to bowls of vegetable and barley soup and as the delicious hot liquid went through me and warmed me and filled me, I felt very happy. It was the sort of happiness that used to flow through me when I'd been riding Why Not, or swimming in the Horseshoe Falls. Easy uncomplicated happiness. The kitchen clock ticked behind me, a mellow hollow tick, and then gathered itself with a clank and a whir to strike eight, giving away as it did so that it was the one that always finished last.

27

Unused to timing the journey, I arrived at school far too early the next morning. The only other person in the classroom was Betty Bougourd and I was about to turn round and go out again when she called me.

'You're good at maths, Nancy.'

'Not very.'

'Better than me. I can't get these problems to come out.' I went unwillingly over to Betty's desk. Since the day I'd knocked her out, we'd given each other a wide berth. 'Every time I do them I get a different answer.' Betty pushed her fat lips out in despair. We were taught maths by Miss Clarkson, who had such an impediment in her speech that we could hardly follow what she was saying. She was very sweet and kind and none of us did well in maths.

'I make the answer to number twenty-five that the tank fills up in three hundred and three hours. That can't be right. It's not as if it's a big tank.'

'It's more like thirty-three hours. I'll check what I got.' As I went to fetch my exercise book, Betty grumbled at the stupidity of the problems.

'I mean, who cares how long a dripping tap takes to fill a tank. Turn the tap off properly or change the washer, is what I say. Right, let's see what you put.' We'd more or less sorted out her answers when Betty said:

'I should watch out for Marion Evans. She really hates you, she's going round saying that you've stolen her best friend. Marion can do some spiteful things to people if she's in the mood.'

'Worse than blowing her nose on my scarf?'

'That was a joke.'

'Funny sort of joke.'

'The trouble with you, Nancy Sykes, is that you go round all high and mighty because of your interesting life in India compared with us poor Guernsey girls and it gets on our nerves sometimes.'

'I don't . . .' I began hotly. 'I don't feel like that at all.'

'I'm not the only one that's said it. People call you Snooty Sykes.'

At this moment a crowd of girls came in and I

left Betty and returned to my desk feeling awful. I found it difficult to concentrate that morning and was relieved I was on library duty at break so I didn't need to talk to any of my class. By lunchtime I was feeling less sore, but I still wondered whether Betty Bougourd was telling the truth. Snooty Sykes. It hurt.

'Nancy! There you are! I've been looking for you all morning!' Stella took my arm as we went into lunch. 'Come into town after school.'

'I can't, Stella. I didn't go home yesterday. I spent the night at my grandparents and I really have to go straight back today.'

'Never mind. By the way, we might be going out in the boat again next Sunday . . . would you like to come?'

I hesitated. I could see Marion Evans sitting at a table at the far end of the hall; she'd clearly saved a place for Stella beside her. The rest of the table was full.

'I'd love to, Stella, but isn't it Marion's turn?'

'She's been plenty of times. It's you I'm asking.' Marion was glaring in our direction.

'I'll let you know. Look, she's saved you a place.' And I went to sit by Elaine Falla, a boring girl with whom I had a dull conversation about the arts and crafts competition held at the end of the term. We had been urged to make things. Elaine was knitting a blanket for her baby sister, pink with a white cat in the middle. I couldn't think of anything to make.

When I arrived back at Maison de Haut, I had the odd sensation of returning home. Sam the black cat was sitting on the mounting block, his paws neatly tucked in and his expression smug. I stroked him and he purred loudly. Then Basil came round the house and gave me a big grin.

'Hi, Nancy, we thought we'd lost you in the storm. I'm just going down to Ted and Flo's . . . want to come? They were asking about you.'

'I've got a lot of homework, Bas, I really can't.'

''Nother time then.' He went off whistling; the cat followed him. Sammy liked going for walks.

Aunt Sophie seemed really pleased to see me; her smile made her face look quite different. She kissed me too, which she hadn't done since I first arrived.

'We missed you. Come and have some tea and tell me what you got up to with my parents.'

'Jigsaws. The one they've just started has three thousand pieces.'

'They're addicts. Their worst deprivation during the war was not having new ones available. Instead they founded a jigsaw club and got everyone they knew swapping jigsaws all round the island. Sometimes the Germans confiscated the jigsaws because they were sure they were a blind to cover something suspicious. Your grandfather loved all that.' She laughed.

Aunt Sophie looked so much happier I asked if she'd heard some good news.

'No, Nancy, no news. But this morning when I woke up I somehow knew I was a widow and it was such a relief accepting it and not fighting against it. I've always refused to believe that Robert is dead, but now something in my bones tells me he is.'

We sat there in silence drinking tea. Marie and

Pierre came in and were surprisingly friendly. My existence at Maison de Haut had turned a corner; even my dark cold bedroom looking more welcoming than usual.

28

'Please would you go round to La Falaise for me,' said Aunt Sophie the following Saturday morning as I was finishing my weekly gorge of fried bacon. 'I haven't had a chance for a couple of weeks.'

It was three weeks since I'd taken the aspirins to the tramp and I hadn't been in that direction since either.

'I'll give you the key, Nancy, so you can check all is well inside. Do you mind going round the empty house on your own?'

'I don't think so,' I said, unsure.

'Take a torch. There's no electricity.' She gave me a large rusty key. 'This opens the back door.' I put it on a piece of string as it was too big for a pocket, hung it round my neck and set off.

It was bitterly cold: everyone kept saying it was unusually cold for late November. Just my luck. I warmed up as I pedalled vigorously to La Falaise, but I was glad I'd got on an old red balaclava helmet of scratchy knitted wool even though I hated wearing it. There was a strong wind blowing over the icy grey sea; the boat trip with the Marquands was cancelled. Stella said there would be no more outings now until the spring.

The silent backyard at La Falaise was growing

tufts of grass between the granite paving stones. The barns had sagging roofs, but there were still some white pigeons living in the pigeon-holes in one end wall. They made a great fluttering of alarm when I biked into the yard.

I pushed the great key into the lock on the back door. There was a scampering sound inside, then silence again. Rats? I tried to peer through the grimy kitchen window, but it was so dark inside I couldn't see much, certainly not the floor. Oh well, rats were preferable to snakes and I'd seen enough snakes close to. It was nice to know they wouldn't be lurking somewhere in the unused house.

I flung the kitchen door open expecting to see rows of malevolent yellow eyes. Dust, droppings, spiders' webs, scuffle marks on the dusty floor . . . but nothing moved as I sent the torch beam into every corner.

The kitchen was just as the old man had left it when he'd gone into hospital: food had been cleared away but that was all. There were still deeply-stained teacups – no saucers – and chipped plates on one corner of the table; things an old man liked to have to hand covered the rest of the table – matches, Epsom Salts, string, a pipe, old news-papers. His tracks to the most used cupboards, both of which hung open, were obvious on the dusty floor. Wood chippings lay everywhere, as if he'd been carving something. I suddenly felt that not only the rats but the old man still inhabited the house and the hair rose on my neck. I forced myself to walk through into the next room, a sort of dining-room that had become a store. Through the dark panelled hall was the parlour, a big room stuffed with old furniture and smelling of dust. There was a round table covered with a plush cloth thickly-powdered with a layer of dust. The room hadn't been used in years. The dust seemed to shine in the beam of my torch.

The thick dust on the cloth was inviting and I started to write my name in it. N . . . A . . . Then I froze.

Tap tap tap. I heard uneven footsteps. Tap tap tap tap. They were in the kitchen and coming closer. Then there was a silence. I could feel my skin tensing; I could hardly breathe. Tap tap. I had to move. I made myself turn and swing the torch into the doorway. Yellow eyes with black slits gleamed at me from the hall.

Daphne, the tramp's goat. Only Daphne. As I let out my pent-up breath Daphne bolted back to the kitchen. I followed and saw the tramp standing in the back doorway. He looked as nervous as I was.

'You frightened me.' I was cross from relief.

'I saw the back door open . . .' The tramp had his bucket full of water beside him. 'Old Mr Jehan lets me fill up at the tap over there. When I saw the open door, I wondered whether he'd got better and come out of hospital.'

'He's too sick to come home. He's sold this house to my parents.'

'Ah.' The tramp picked his bucket up. 'So they'll be moving in soon.'

'No . . . not yet.' I didn't know how much to tell him. 'But I'm sure they wouldn't mind you taking water when you need it.'

'Thank you.' The tramp started to cough, a terrible racking cough that made him drop the bucket and lean against the door post. He spat into a piece of torn cloth doing service as a hanky and I'm sure I saw blood.

'Did you get the aspirin?'

'So it was you,' he wheezed, before another attack of coughing wrenched him. He could hardly stand up, his body was so shaken, so I pushed a chair under him. Daphne watched us with her unwinking yellow eyes.

'Do you need more?'

'I bought some, thank you.'

It seemed to me his illness needed more help than an aspirin. 'You ought to go to a doctor.'

'No doctor.' He was getting his breath back, but he still looked terrible.

'Let me carry your bucket for you back to the bunker.'

We set off for the bunker after I'd locked up. The poor man walked very slowly; Daphne had lots of time for grazing. The wind bit into us.

When I put the bucket down outside the bunker, the tramp said: 'Would you be so kind as to come in?' There was nothing I wanted less, but I felt I couldn't refuse. I picked up the bucket again and followed him in after he'd tethered Daphne.

The lower room of the solid concrete bunker had a narrow slit for a window, over which some sacking was hung. The tramp lit a candle. I saw a bed made of blankets on drift-wood planks raised on stones and a tea-chest for a table. More drift-wood and stones formed some shelving, on which was the tramp's meagre store of food. The place smelled more of sea and salt and the paraffin for the primus than of dirt; even his smell wasn't too bad: there was a sea-salt, sea-weedy undertone that made it bearable.

'I haven't had my tea,' croaked the tramp, sitting on the bed. 'If you boil up the billy we can both have some.'

So I found myself clumsily lighting his primus and putting two cupfuls of water into the tin pot he called his billy. His tea and sugar and other dry supplies were in an odd collection of bottles and boxes he'd obviously picked up on the beach. Hanging from nails in the walls were more of his finds: dried seaweed in fantastic twisted forms, fishermen's dark green glass balls still enclosed in their netting, pieces of bark or wood smoothed and worked by the sea into strange shapes. As I was looking at these while waiting for his billy to boil, he began to recite in a croaking whisper:

> Full fathom five thy father lies
> Of his bones are coral made
> Those are pearls that were his eyes
> Nothing of him that doth fade
> Both doth suffer a sea change—

He broke off and started coughing again, terrible coughs.

'You should see a doctor, you know.'

He shook his head while he coughed; by the time the bout of coughing stopped the billy was boiling and I realized I'd have to make his tea. It's a feeble thing to admit, but I'd never made a cup of tea in my life.

'How much tea shall I put?'

'Bring it here.' He put a pinch of tea into each

chipped cup and I poured water on it. 'What I like is condensed milk in my tea. There's some left in that tin. Plenty for us both.'

So I stirred the sticky white stuff into the tea and watched the leaves swirl. Then the tramp started to sip his noisily, cradling the cup in his hands. I tried mine and found it very good.

'Are you a poet, then?'

'Poet?'

'You were saying some poetry weren't you, about a sea change?'

'That's not my poetry. I can't write poetry. No, that was Shakespeare.'

'You've finished your tea. Do you want another?'

'Put the billy on again. I get so cold these days.'

'How do you manage here when it's really bad outside? Snowing?'

But he didn't answer. He hadn't heard me; he was staring blankly at the wall, muttering the Shakespeare again. I sat down on the tea-chest when I'd put some more water on to boil.

When I gave him his second cup of tea, he said: 'So old Jehan has sold his house. Is he dead?'

'No, but he won't ever be leaving the hospital.'

'Poor sod. I'd rather die anywhere than in a prison. What did you say your name was?'

'Nancy.'

'Nancy, that's right. A yankee name. But you're not a yankee, I can tell. You're a Guernsey girl. A Guernesaise.'

'Half English, half Guernsey.'

'Or Sarnian. The Romans called this island Sarnia.'

'Are you Sarnian then?'

'No questions. I don't like questions, people ask too many of them.'

'You ask questions too. You asked my name. You should tell me yours in exchange. All I know is that your goat is called Daphne.'

'Daphne never asks or answers questions. Perfect company.'

'I'll go then.' I was tired of his evasions.

'Don't be angry. I didn't say you weren't good company too.'

'I have to go anyway. My aunt will be expecting me home.'

He started another coughing fit, more terrible than the last. He had to lie down flat when it was over, he was so shattered by it.

I stared uselessly at him. 'Is there anything else I can do?'

He shook his head and shut his eyes as if he was about to sleep. I made my way up the stairs and checked that Daphne was properly tethered. She stood eyeing me from the top of a rock as I walked back to La Falaise.

29

The next day I decided I'd go to Stella's via the tramp's bunker, long way round though it was. It was even colder; the sky was a bowl of icy white . . . it was like being in a fridge. I took a piece of stale cake and a Guernsey biscuit, also stale, and filled the biscuit – really a sort of flat roll – with dripping. I took a few apples and a swede from a pile in the shed. Aunt Sophie was wandering around, still in her church clothes, so I couldn't take much. It never occurred to me to ask her help over the tramp; I somehow felt she had enough troubles of her own, I suppose.

Daphne was tethered in a different spot, so at least the tramp had been out.

'It's me, Nancy,' I called as I went down to the lower room in the bunker. He was huddled on the makeshift bed; the sacking over the gun emplacement slot had slipped so light and cold air came in. 'It's Nancy,' I repeated when he didn't open his eyes. 'How are you?'

'No better, no worse,' he whispered. 'Make some tea, girl.' He looked worse.

So I put the billy on to boil and fetched another bucket of water from La Falaise. Then I opened the bag of food and unwrapped the Guernsey biscuit.

'Sit up. Here's your tea and I've brought you some food.' He struggled upright, his beard pressed into a funny shape from the way he'd been lying. He peered at me out of bloodshot eyes. 'Look, I've brought you a Guernsey biscuit with some dripping inside.'

He took the pale brown circle of bread with its customary ring of dents in the top and gazed at it entranced.

'A Guernsey biscuit. I haven't seen one of those since before the war.'

'I hope you like them.'

To my horror tears began to pour from his eyes. They coursed down his cheeks as he stared at the biscuit, which he raised almost to his lips.

He looked as if he was going to kiss it.

'Eat it, it'll give you strength.' I went off to make his tea the way he liked it. I wished he'd stop crying, but I could hear he hadn't. At last he began to eat the wretched biscuit and his tears stopped.

'I can't come again until next week-end,' I said rather brusquely. 'Will you be all right? Do you need anything?'

'I need more aspirin and cough mixture. The nearest chemist is in St Martin's and I can't walk there like this.'

'I'll buy them for you. And I could get a doctor to call . . .'

'No doctors. I told you that already. Fetch me that tin, would you? That black one, yes.'

It was an old tea-caddy; its contents rattled and rustled, and turned out to be money. Quite a fair amount of money. The tramp took half a crown and gave it to me.

'You don't leave this tin lying around, do you? It might get stolen.'

'It has a very good hiding place. Not even a clever girl like you could find it.'

As I bicycled away towards Stella's house, I wondered if he was the sort of madman who is stinking rich really, but who can't bear to live with it.

30

Stella wound the gramophone up again and put the needle back to the beginning of 'Little Brown Jug' for the umpteenth time. After the usual scraping noise the cheerful bouncy tune filled the room and we were off. Stella was teaching me to dance.

Stella lived in a bungalow near Saint's Bay in St Martin's. It had a keyhole door and a garden full of weeds all round it. A row of well-kept sheds housed Bill Marquand's carrier pigeons, but his greenhouses were as ramshackle as his garden. Inside, the house was incredibly untidy; there were tottering heaps of things on every surface. The Marquands obviously lived without putting anything away. Cupboards yawned open showing bare shelves inside. The only tidy thing was the big gramophone in its wooden cabinet; a neat row of those dear little tins of needles with the white dog listening to his master's voice on each lid lay on a ledge beside the turntable and the records were carefully stored in their paper sleeves.

Bill's head came round the door when we put on 'Chatanooga Choo Choo'.

'Always Glenn Miller, Stella. Let's have a change, for God's sake.' I stopped dancing but Stella went on twirling round the room. 'Why don't you play that Danny Kaye record I gave you?'

'Can't dance to it.'

'You and your mother are impossible. I don't know what I've done to deserve it.' He disappeared.

'Mum loves Glenn Miller too and she's a really good dancer. She taught me.' Stella sank into an armchair, I into a sofa. 'Dad refuses to dance. So she keeps in practice by dancing with me.'

I loved being in Stella's house, it was so different from any home I'd ever been in. I couldn't imagine my mother or Aunt Sophie spending hours doing the quickstep and the foxtrot with their daughters.

'You'd be good, too, Nancy, if only you'd relax a bit.'

'Give me time. Help, talking of time, is that clock right?'

'More or less.'

'Then I must go. I promised my aunt I'd be back at six.'

'I'll come as far as Les Caches with you, to see you on your way.'

As we biked along, an old man in his front garden reminded me of the tramp and I told Stella about him.

'But if he's so ill he might die, living in that freezing bunker.'

'That's what's worrying me. And he refuses to see a doctor. He was angry when I mentioned it.'

'Who is he, anyway? What's his name?'

'I've no idea. He never tells me, he just avoids questions. He's really strange. He's certainly sick in his body, he could well be sick in his mind too. Yet sometimes he talks quite normally.'

'You oughtn't to go and see him on your own, Nancy.'

'He's not frightening at all. He's kind. Just strange, like I said. But I really don't know what to do, Stella. If he dies and I haven't called a doctor I'll feel like a murderer. But if I call the doctor and he gets taken away from the life he's chosen, I'll feel terrible too.'

'I suppose if he really wants to be left the way he is, we ought to respect that.'

'I agree.' We free-wheeled in silence for a while. 'He coughs blood, Stella.'

'Ugh. Listen. Why don't you ask your aunt to come with you next time you go? He couldn't get angry since she's not a doctor. She'd be able to help you decide.'

'Perhaps I will ask her. She's been a bit more cheerful recently, maybe she won't mind giving her time.'

'Definitely ask her. I think the whole business sounds too serious for you to manage on your own.'

On the way back I decided I'd wait until I'd taken the tramp his medicines. If he was no better, or worse, I'd have to get help.

31

'Would you like these Guernsey sweets? I've got more than I need.'

'Oh, Grand-mère, how lovely. I made the mistake of spending all my sweet ration on Clear Gums and now I'm sick of them.' I'd undone the tubes and collected the sweets into their colours; the heaps of black, red, orange, yellow and green looked so pretty on my bedspread I'd kept them separate, putting each colour into a jamjar. Then of course I'd eaten the ones I liked first and was left with a jar full of green and a few yellow ones mixed in. By the end of the week I never wanted to taste another Clear Gum.

Guernsey sweets are made like pillows covered with thin stripes; fruit ones of various colours, pinkish clove ones, redder aniseed, black liquorice, all covered with fine white stripes and wrapped in clear cellophane. I didn't much like the clove or aniseed, but as Grand-mère preferred those, we divided the sweets up very satisfactorily.

'Now, show me the letter from your parents that came yesterday.'

Grand-mère and I were in the drawing-room, me as usual on the footstool by her chair. She put on her half-moon glasses and read the letter out loud for Grand-père's benefit as well.

> On board the Strathmore, one day away
> from Port Said. November 8.

Darling Nancy,

We think about you constantly and hope you're settling in. We are still sad we didn't have a chance to talk to you that last afternoon in England . . . where on earth were you? Sophie said she had seen you five minutes before and she couldn't understand where you'd got to. She said she thought you were still homesick for India and that was why you disappeared for hours at a time. We told her you used to do that in Assam too . . . remember the hours you used to spend in that tree-house? It must be nice to have Bahyong's model of it with you in Guernsey. Dear Bahyong, it will be lovely to see him and the other servants again.

I explained to my grandparents who Bahyong was and promised to show them the model next time they visited Maison de Haut. For a while Grand-mère gazed over my head, dreaming, and then with a jolt went back to the letter.

Our trip has been uneventful so far. Even the Bay of Biscay wasn't rough and it has been absolutely lovely weather crossing the Mediterranean, blue blue skies and a nice bracing bite to the air. Lots of dolphins. How lovable they are, with their snub playful faces. Remember the one that kept up with the old *City of Exeter* for miles and miles? I think it must have found us again, because the same thing has just happened!

Clare is being very good, ever so much better than she was when going Home. I think being an 'only' child so to speak has put her on her mettle. She certainly misses you. She says 'Nancy' every time she sees your photograph – we've got it out in the cabin, on the shelf beside the basin.

How is school? I hope you haven't knocked any more people out and that the dreaded Miss Porrit is also behaving herself. Mind you, she's someone to whom that cliché applies, that her bark is worse than her bite.

I had the strange impression as the letter was read out that a long time had passed since my parents had left; perhaps it was hearing their words read out by a new voice, but I couldn't help feeling they were far away in time as well as space. And it occurred to me that my parents' picture of my life in Guernsey was already shadowy and out of date. I felt a little ripple of inner excitement. I was on my own and I was coping.

32

This feeling was firmly banished by the end of the week. I caught a cold which was made worse because I got drenched bicycling home from school. On Friday I woke up feeling so ill I could hardly stagger down the staircase – freezing cold stone under my bare feet – and tell Aunt Sophie I couldn't go to school.

'Go back to bed.' She felt my hot forehead. 'You've got a temperature. I'll bring your breakfast up to you.'

When she arrived Sammy the cat was following her. He jumped on the bed and sniffed at my porridge.

'Get out, cat!' said Aunt Sophie sharply, pushing him aside.

'No, no, I'd like him here, let him stay . . .' But it was too late; rebuffed, Sammy stalked out of my door. 'Puss, puss, come back.'

'He's buzzed off downstairs,' said my aunt and the latch clicked down as the door shut behind her.

So I was left alone in my dark bedroom with a head as thick as the steaming porridge in front of me and an aching heart. It wasn't just the lack of Sammy for company. Being ill made me realize how much I still missed my old life and how fragile my hold was on my new one.

I ate a little of my porridge, drank the tea and then lay there, miserable in every atom of my being. The house around me was now silent.

Mum, Dad, Clare, Congreeal, Laughing, Rinjo, Bahyong, Ahmed, Guru, Purram Das, Abdul . . . their absence was like toothache. When I'd been ill at home in Shillong I was never alone unless I was asleep. Congreeal would have been constantly around, calm and comforting; the mosquito nets would be lifted and tied up so that the bed seemed to have white wings. I could look out on to the veranda; I could hear the myna saying 'hullo, hullo'. I could hear the whir of Ahmed's sewing machine, a rich, nutty noise because it rested on the wooden floor. In the distance was the high-pitched singing of Happy the sweeper as he brushed the paths. Horses' hooves on the drive told me my parents had come back from their early morning ride. I heard them dismount and talk to the syce; then my mother would come up the veranda steps into my room.

'Hullo, poppet. You look a little better, doesn't she, Congreeal? What about some fresh orange juice and a nice dish of sliced papayas and mangoes and bananas for breakfast . . . does that appeal to you?'

Oh, the smell of that freshly sliced fruit in the little green glass bowl on a tray on my lap; oh, the smells in the background of thatch and betel-nut and tropical wood and spices and that special wax polish used on the furniture and the dhobi-washed sheets that smelled so different from these Guernsey ones which had a whiff of bonfire about them because they'd been hung out to dry too near the smoke.

I lay there in the silent house, hearing only the grandfather clock striking at half past and on the hour and felt more unhappy than at any time since my parents left.

*

When I woke up hours later, Sammy the cat was a dead weight on my feet. My door was shut, so Aunt Sophie must have persuaded him to return. I was delighted to see him, but didn't make the mistake of showing him how pleased I was. I tickled his ears and he slept on. The house was still silent; then the grandfather clock gathered itself with a whirring noise and struck twelve. I was amazed at how long I'd slept; I still felt ill, but the acute misery and homesickness had passed.

Soon my aunt brought me some soup and then stood uneasily beside me as she took my temperature.

'Nearly a hundred and one. I think I'll get the doctor if it isn't down by this evening. By the way, I found these in the hall in a paper bag. You don't have to buy your own medicines, you know.' Aunt Sophie took the aspirins and cough mixture I'd bought for the tramp from her apron pocket. I'd completely forgotten about him.

'They're not for me, Aunt Sophie. I . . . I got them for an old man who lives near La Falaise. He asked me to get them for him, he wasn't well enough to get to St Martin's himself. I'll take them to him at the week-end.'

'Not this week-end, Nancy. You're not well enough yourself. You can't go bicycling around for a few days.'

'If you go over in the car, perhaps I could come too if I was well wrapped up?'

'We'll see. Who is the old man?'

'I don't know his name—' The telephone started shrilling at that moment, and my aunt went off, leaving the medicines on my dressing-table. I tucked them away so that they were less obvious and when my aunt returned she'd forgotten about them.

Why didn't I ask her to take the medicines to the tramp, I wondered afterwards. I suppose I was afraid she'd be angry that I'd involved myself with a strange old man who might be dangerous. I considered asking Basil to do it for me, but for much the same reason I felt unwilling. Besides, I was sure they would report the tramp to the police or certainly to a doctor and end his precarious way of living. I knew my tramp would prefer to do without his aspirins and cough mixture than have strangers marching in with doctors and policemen.

'Suffer a sea change' . . . I couldn't remember any of the poem except those words. I dozed off, and dreamed of a little boat sailing away with the tramp and Daphne sitting merrily in it as the boat scudded along, surrounded by dolphins over the still, warm seas.

33

By five o'clock the next day, Saturday, I was allowed to get up because I was feeling so much better. The fire was lit in the parlour specially for me and I sat curled up in my eiderdown reading *Lorna Doone* and feeling very cosy. The small fire flickered and threw shadows round the room; rain beat against the windows and the gale force wind shrieked outside.

'What a night. So you're not going to die yet, I see.' Basil came in and flicked me on the head before going to the piano. Agnes followed and shut the door.

'How are you then, Nancy?' She went and sat on the mat in front of the fire.

'Much better.'

'Good. Let's have some music, Bas. Play some boogie-woogie.'

'Are you sure Mum's gone out?'

'I saw her leave for the Guillemettes. She said she'd be half an hour.'

Basil played everything by ear; he only had to hear a tune once and he could play it in any key and jazz it up.

'You're so good, Bas. Will you teach me?'

'I couldn't teach the cat to play, Nancy. I do it all instinctively, as Dad did. I just hear the tunes in my head and out they come.'

'I can't play like him; it's very unfair.' Agnes lay flat out, stretching her slim body. 'I started lessons before the war, but they had to come to an end because my teacher was evacuated.' She stared upwards while her brother filled the room with bouncing sound. 'God, the war was awful.'

'What was worst about it?'

'Not so much all the obvious things, but the fact that nobody knew when it was all going to end. For a year we kept thinking it couldn't go on much longer, even the Germans were getting desperate, but month after month it dragged on. I began to think that Bas and I would miss out completely on all the ordinary things teenagers like doing, parties, fun, all that.' She rolled over and propped herself on her elbows. Her teeth shone white as she grinned at me in the light of the fire. 'Mind you, we're all making up for it now. We can go to a dozen different places every week-end to have fun. And now there's the Barn Club, it's even better.'

'What goes on at the Barn Club?'

'Oh, just dancing, talking, music, nothing special in one sense. What's good is the atmosphere . . . we run the Club ourselves the way we want it.'

'One of the rules is you have to be sixteen to join.' Basil did some crashing chords. 'But I'm sure you'll be in there, Nancy, the minute you're sixteen.'

The latch clicked, the door opened and Aunt Sophie stood there. Basil stopped playing at once.

'Sorry, Mum, I thought you were down at Le Puit.'

'I met Flo in the lane, going out, so I came straight back. Go on playing, Basil.' He sat at the piano with his hands still. 'Play if you want to. I've been very unreasonable about that piano.' She went out again quickly, without shutting the door.

'Well, well.' Basil played a few notes quietly.

Agnes leapt to her feet, her eyes alight. 'Play "Little Brown Jug", go on. Mum likes that.' Basil played a few notes, then got up and closed the piano.

'I was going to stop anyway. It's time I got moving. See you later, Agnes. I'll be at the Club about ten.'

Agnes wandered aimlessly about the room for a bit after he'd gone. 'It's been too bloody much,' she suddenly burst out. 'First all the uncertainty not knowing when the Occupation was going to end and then on top of that two years after the war's all over we still don't know what's happened to Dad!'

Alone again in the room, I drew my eiderdown

more closely about me and stared for a long time into the fire.

34

Stella came to see me on Sunday. It was her first visit to Maison de Haut and she came without warning me. When I saw her looking hesitantly round the yard I shouted her name for joy.

'Stella!' I tore open the kitchen door. 'Stella!'

'You don't look sick at all. I was expecting to find you languishing in bed.'

'I'm much better today. Back to school tomorrow.'

'Marie seemed to think you'd be off for days when I asked her on Friday.'

'It's good to see you.' We stood awkwardly at the back door chatting until Aunt Sophie called from the kitchen.

'Where are your manners, Nancy? Bring your friend in and shut the door.'

'This is Stella Marquand, Aunt Sophie.'

'Hullo, Stella. Which Marquands do you come from, the Hougue Fougue or the Saints?'

'From Saints. My Dad's Bill Marquand. He knows you, Mrs Le Patourel, he came here once to buy seedlings. He told me how to find this house.'

'Bill the Blight,' said Aunt Sophie, smiling. 'Does he still have his pigeons?'

'Yes. And plenty of blight in his greenhouses.'

Aunt Sophie laughed. After a few more remarks

about Marquands in general, I managed to get Stella away and up to my room.

'I thought you said your aunt was a real misery.'

'She's much better now . . . she's really cheered up recently.'

'Where are all your cousins?'

'No idea. Out and about.'

'What's that?' Stella pointed to the model of my tree-house. I explained and she looked over Bahyong's baby tree-house with an odd expression on her face.

'How big's the real one?'

'I could stand up in it and invite a couple of friends in too.' I described the tree-house in more detail and told her about the last tea party and its failure. Stella kept the model in her hands as I talked, opening its little windows and stroking the thatch.

'I tell you, Nancy, I hadn't realized until now how lucky you were to be born and brought up in India. I've never seen such a wonderful tree-house, for a start. It's like the dream of every child.'

'No-one else in Shillong had one like it either.'

'Tell me about your life there, Nancy. You hardly ever talk about it. Go on, tell me.'

We talked and talked until it was nearly dark and Stella had to leave and bicycle home. As she was about to go out of the gate she remembered the tramp.

'Was he all right?'

'I haven't seen him since I spoke to you. I'll have to go next week-end with his medicines.'

'I could have gone for you today.'

'I didn't think of it.'

'Never mind, he sounds as if he's used to a hard life. He's probably got better without the aspirins and cough mixture . . . they wouldn't have made much difference anyway.'

'I expect you're right. 'Bye, Stella, thanks a million for coming. See you tomorrow.'

'*A la prochaine.*'

35

It grew colder and colder during the next week. I wore all my vests and both my school jumpers on top of each other and still felt cold by the end of the day. The coal stove in our classroom gave off very little heat unless you were sitting right by it, which I wasn't. My desk was not only a long way from it, but I was near the big sash windows which rattled loosely in the wind. I froze. No-one else seemed to feel the cold as I did, so they were not particularly sympathetic. I didn't expect them to be and so it was surprisingly nice when Betty Bougourd came to school with a pair of fingerless gloves for me.

'My mum knits them for me. I don't need this pair, I've got two already.' Betty was offhand. My knuckles felt snug within minutes.

'No gloves for games. Off with them, Nancy,' shouted Miss Hampton as we stood in the freezing wind waiting to start hockey.

'These aren't really gloves—'

'You can't hold a hockey stick with your palms full of wool. Come on, off with them. Run hard, Nancy, you'll soon warm up.'

How I hated Miss Hampton and hockey and cold mud on my blue knees and bumps from that iron ball on my shins.

'Helen was wonderful at hockey. She was captain of the first eleven. It's funny you don't take after her at all,' said my aunt. 'What did you play in India?'

'Volley-ball and tennis and badminton. But I wasn't very good; I don't seem to hit balls easily. They just hit me. Look at the bruise I got in hockey.'

'Poor Nancy. By the way, while I remember, Grand-mère rang up today and suggested that you spend one night a week with them. If you'd like to do that, decide which day suits you and give her a ring.' Aunt Sophie was kneading dough vigorously.

'Would you mind me going?'

'Of course not, Nancy. I think it's a good idea. They obviously like you, or they wouldn't have asked you. Actually, I was quite surprised. My mother doesn't often put herself out for the young.'

36

It was still freezing cold at the week-end. I knew I had to go and see the old tramp in his icy concrete bunker on the cliffs and shivered as I thought of it. Snug in my balaclava and thick coat and trousers tucked into my boots, I set off down the lane on my bike. When I passed Le Puit, Ted was on a bank sawing at some branches.

'Hullo, Helen's Nancy! How are you?'

'Hullo, Ted! I'm fine!' I whizzed on, suddenly filled for a moment with that sort of happiness which I usually connected only with India . . .

Breakers crashed along the edge of Rocquaine Bay. Plumes of spray rose as the sea surged against wall or rock. Seagulls cried and pebbles roared and rattled in the undertow. I stopped at the little causeway leading to Fort Grey and there, in the flotsam, I saw a green shiny thing gleaming amongst all the weed and broken wood.

A green glass fisherman's ball. I'd been longing to find one. Basil told me they weren't so common now because the fishermen were turning to more modern ways of floating their nets. I picked it up carefully. It was a beautiful pale bluey-green, much lighter than the usual dark bottle green of most balls. I held it up in delight and slipped it into my saddle-bag where it clinked against the bottle of cough mixture. To keep them apart, I went back for more flotsam – a piece of tree-root, smoothed and whitened like bone, some dried seaweed stems twisted into corkscrew curls, a piece of cork bark. The sea beat and sucked at the pebbles all round me; I saw an empty pop bottle floating at the edge and rescued it – you got a penny deposit back on these. It was scratched, as if it had rolled about at the edge of a rough sea for some time.

I was just putting off what I had to do next. I went on beachcombing because I was nervous . . . no, frightened . . . of what I might find at the bunker. Eventually when my saddle-bag could hold no more, I bicycled up the steep hill that led to La Falaise just below the brow of the headland.

First I looked at La Falaise. Everything was the

same; the only thing odd I noticed was the outdoor tap dripping, so I turned it off more firmly. Then, feeling my legs going slower and slower, I made for the bunker.

I could hear Daphne bleating. At first I couldn't find her, then I saw she was tethered further down the cliff below the bunker. She bleated again when she saw me. She'd eaten the cliff bare all round her. She stared up at me with those disturbing yellow eyes and bleated again.

'You'll have to wait, Daphne.'

Now I had to enter the bunker. Aspirins in one hand, cough mixture in the other, I made myself start down the staircase.

'Hullo!' No reply.

Perhaps he was dead. I had seen dead bodies in India, they were commonplace out there. But they'd been distant, nothing to do with me. The tramp was different. I went slowly on down the stairs.

The sacking over the gun-slit was loose and flapping in the wind. In the half light I could see the tramp curled up on his bed, quite still. I crept up to him, my heart beating so hard it seemed audible.

'Hullo,' I whispered again. 'Are you all right?' Which was a silly question, but what else could I say?

No reply. Then his head moved very slightly. I touched his shoulder, then his hand. It was very cold, so cold that if he hadn't moved his head, I might have taken him for dead.

'I've brought you your medicines,' I said, close to his ear. 'I'll make you some tea.' He gave a faint, faint groan. My hands shaking, I lit the primus and looked for water. There was none. 'I'll be back in a second with more water.'

Running to La Falaise and back got my blood racing and my brain working. Apart from anything else, the man was dying of cold. His hands were nearly as cold as the granite all round me. He was probably desperately ill as well. A hot drink could only be a good thing and then I would have to go and get a doctor and an ambulance or he would surely die.

The water took ages to boil. I tried to get him to say something while it was boiling, but all he could do was groan. I made the tea, propped his matted head up and spooned in the hot drink. He swallowed it eagerly and I felt encouraged. I made him a second cup and started to give it to him when he opened his eyes and tried to speak.

'What is it?'

'Daphne.'

'She's all right, she's outside.'

'Move her, give her water.'

'Of course I will. Drink some more.'

'Daphne.' He shut his mouth and I had to go then and there to see to his goat. I moved her back on top of the headland and put her in the corner of a field that probably belonged to someone but I was past caring. It had long thick grass and poor Daphne buried her face in it. I left a tin of water near her and hurried back after I'd tied her tether securely to a gorse-root.

The tramp had his eyes open when I went down again.

'I brought you some bread and cheese.' He didn't answer, so I put the sandwich beside him.

'I'm going off to fetch a doctor now. If I don't, you'll surely die.'

He still did not answer, but I could see he'd heard me. I tacked up the sacking to keep out the wind and wrapped his blankets securely round him. From the smell, he'd wet his bed at some point, but it seemed dry again now.

'Listen, I'll be back as soon as I can. Daphne's eating away in a new place, she's fine now.'

He whispered something which could have been thanks and shut his eyes again. I rushed off and rode back to Maison de Haut so fast I was dripping with sweat when I arrived. The house was empty.

'Gone to Town with Marie and Pierre. Help yourself to the bubble and squeak in the lower oven. Basil's down at Le Puit. Love Aunt S.

The note lay on the kitchen table in the silent house. I wanted to weep. They were clearly gone for hours, a whole day's shopping. Le Puit. I'd go down and ask Basil and the Guillemettes. Back I jumped on my bike, banging and scraping my shin as I did so. The pain was such that I free-wheeled all the way down to Le Puit.

Basil was crossing the yard as I rode in. He was carrying wooden trays filled with bulbs and they looked heavy. He managed a wink in my direction as he hurried into an open shed. I followed him.

'Bas, there's an old tramp with a goat who wanders about Rocquaine . . . he's terribly ill and needs to go to hospital. I came to get him a doctor, but no-one's at home.'

'What old tramp? Where is he?'

'In his bunker . . . one of the German bunkers on the cliff at Pleinmont.'

'How on earth did you find him in the first place?'

'I took him some medicines. But he'll die, Bas, if something isn't done. I don't even know the name of a doctor.'

'You'd better get hold of old Rabey. He's the family doctor.' But Basil didn't move. Then Ted came in with another pile of bulb trays.

'Nancy wants to call Doctor Rabey to go and see some old tramp.'

'The one with the goat—' I began.

'That old rascal.' Ted picked over bulbs, whistling through his few teeth.

'He's going to die, Ted, if he doesn't get to hospital soon.' I was beginning to feel a bit desperate.

'Those old boys are very tough, they're used to a hard life.' Ted started re-stacking trays. I wanted to shake him. I turned to Basil.

'Give me the 'phone number and I'll ring the doctor myself. If we don't do anything we'll be murderers.'

'Trouble is, little one, old Rabey's not likely to take much notice of a child ringing him up. He's a bad-tempered old cuss at the best of times and Saturday afternoon is not the best of times. Hand me that last tray, would you, Bas?'

'Please help me, *please*.' I couldn't stop tears coming to my eyes. 'The old man's so ill. When I found him I thought he was dead already. We must hurry, please hurry . . .'

Ted stopped his work abruptly. 'Right. Come

into the house. We'll get Flo to ring the doctor, she's got a way with Rabey. You go and tell her all the details. Where is this old fellow?'

'In a bunker on the cliff near La Falaise.'

'It must be bloody freezing in there.'

'It is.'

We went into the low stone-flagged kitchen with a big pump by the door. Flo was peeling apples with a Siamese cat on her lap. We explained the problem and she transferred the cat to her neck like a collar while she went off to 'phone Rabey.

'Bas, I suggest you take our car and drive over with Nancy, take the old boy some blankets. He must have hypothermia by now on top of everything else.'

'Some hot water bottles would help him too.'

'We've only got the old stone ones but they keep hot a good long time.'

A huge kettle was hissing gently on the range, half boiling; Ted fetched the stone jars from a cupboard.

'There you are girl, fill 'em up. I expect Flo's got some soup in the larder. Warm that up and take it in a thermos.'

Flo came back, the little cat still round her neck. 'Rabey's not on call today, but his locum is young Jim Le Tissier. People tell me he's very good.'

'Better than Rabey,' said Basil. 'Can't see the old boy enjoying a trip to a smelly old bunker.'

'It's not too smelly.'

'Glad to hear it.' Bas didn't look very enthusiastic about our visit. 'When's Le Tissier getting there?'

'I said to meet you at La Falaise . . . he said he'd

be there at two-thirty. It's half past one now . . .
have you had lunch yet, Nancy?'

'No, but it doesn't matter . . . I'm not hungry.'

'We've had ours, but you must eat something
before you rush off. I'll make you a beef sandwich.
Sit down, girl. I'll do those bottles in a minute.'

37

Ten minutes later Basil and I drove off to Pleinmont
loaded with warm things for the sick man.

'What's his name?'

'I don't know.'

'Can't think why I'm doing this. I'm useless with
sick people.' Basil drove Ted's old car with extreme
care, very slowly. 'These gears are the devil,' he said
after the car made nasty grating noises.

'If you park in the yard at La Falaise we can
carry the stuff to the cliff path. There'll be time to
take a load before the doctor comes.'

Loaded with heavy stone bottles, Basil followed
me to the bunker. I carried the rest. Daphne jumped
up on a bank and bleated at us when she heard our
voices.

'That's his goat. There's another problem if he
has to go to hospital.'

Basil didn't reply. I led the way down the steps
in the bunker, calling, 'Hullo, I'm back,' as I did so.
The old tramp was lying exactly as I'd left him. His
sandwich was untouched.

'*Damn de bougre*,' said Basil, looking round.
Somehow the smell had got worse:

'We've brought you some hot water bottles,' I said to the tramp. His eyes flickered open, then shut again. I put one bottle between his hands and the others against his back and stomach. It was pointless putting one at his feet because he still had his boots on. 'And some hot soup. Would you like some now?'

The matted head turned slightly towards us. The eyes fluttered open again.

'Spoon some in,' he croaked.

'Put a rolled-up blanket under his head, Bas.' Basil hadn't moved; he was staring wordlessly at the old man. I took a blanket from the heap and slipped it behind the tramp's filthy head. He probably had lice. Oh well. I found his spoon and opened the vacuum flask full of delicious-smelling soup. Basil was being useless, standing as frozen as the figure on the bed. 'Hold this bowl, Bas, would you?'

'It's Dad. I think it's Dad,' he whispered.

'What?' I spilt some of the soup. 'What do you mean?'

'Put that down a minute and come outside.' Basil almost dragged me up the steps. He was shaking. 'That man looks like my father. If it isn't Robert Le Patourel, it's his double.'

'It can't be.'

'His eyes are the same, his nose. Dad's got a little round mole near his nose, so has that man. Here.' Basil pointed to his own face. 'It's a funny place to have a mole. Even his voice sounds right. But he looks far too old. Dad would only be fifty now.' We stared in silence at each other.

'I suppose if someone hasn't had a bath or a

haircut for years they would look old,' I said slowly. 'His hair seems grey, but it's so dirty and long and matted it's hard to tell the real colour.'

'Something tells me that's my father.' Basil looked so pale he was nearly green. 'I can't help it, I'm going to be sick. You go back to him.' He dashed off round the bunker. I returned to the tramp, still finding it impossible that Basil could be right.

I spooned soup into his mouth and looked at the mole by his nose. When he'd had a couple of good mouthfuls, I asked: 'Is your name Robert Le Patourel?'

'No.' I offered him more soup, but he went on muttering.

'I have no name. I suffered a sea change and have no name.'

I heard Basil coming down the steps.

'He says he isn't Robert Le Patourel.'

'Those are pearls that were his eyes.'

'He's delirious, by the sound of it. Nancy, it's nearly two-thirty, the doctor will be arriving at La Falaise any minute. He'll go away if he finds no-one there. I'd better go and meet him.' But Basil did not move; he could not take his eyes off the tramp.

'OK, you go.'

'I . . . oh, God!' Basil ran off up the steps again.

During all this the tramp hadn't opened his eyes. Now he wouldn't open his lips either, so I put the soup aside and started putting more blankets on him. He was breathing very hoarsely, as if breath was being painfully dragged out of his lungs. He muttered something.

'More soup?'

'Is Daphne all right?'

205

'She's happy on a fresh patch of grass.'

'She should have come in at night. I've been too ill to fetch her.'

'Don't worry about her. I'll look after her when you're in hospital.'

'Hospital? I don't want to go to hospital.'

'You're too ill to stay here.'

He groaned and turned away. The hot water bottle rolled from his hands and landed with a clunk on the concrete floor. I gave it back to him and looked again at that mole and the grimy skin round his closed eyes. Perhaps he wasn't very old, perhaps he was fifty, perhaps he was . . .

Crisp footsteps came down the stairs and a strange young man appeared, followed by a tense-looking Basil.

'I'm Doctor Le Tissier.' The doctor went over to the tramp and bent over him. 'I've been asked to take a look at you.' The tramp did not move. 'If you'd let me begin by taking your temperature and your pulse—'

'Bugger off!' The tramp's hoarse shout made us jump. 'Just bugger off . . . *fous le camp.*'

'No. I can't leave a man as sick as you are untended.'

'Bugger off,' whispered the tramp, less convincingly. But when Doctor Le Tissier tried to take his pulse, the tramp swung his fist and hit the doctor on the nose.

'Don't be such a bloody fool.' Angry, the doctor grabbed hold of both hands and the tramp was so weak after his effort that he didn't struggle. 'At least let me take your pulse and your temperature. You don't have to accept my diagnosis and you don't have to go to hospital should I suggest it, but since I'm here I'm not going until I've examined you.'

So the tramp meekly allowed the thermometer to be put in his mouth and the doctor listened to his wheezing chest. The smell emanating from the tramp was awful now. I began to feel frightened of what would happen if he refused to move from the bunker. I went and stood by Basil, who put his arm round me. He was still shaking slightly, but perhaps it was from the cold.

'That man is so like my father I can't believe he's telling the truth when he says he's not Robert Le Patourel,' Basil whispered.

'Tell him who you are. He hasn't seen you properly, I don't think he registered you at all. Go up close, see if he recognizes you.'

'The trouble is, it's seven years since he last saw me, or I him. I could be wrong. But he *sounds* like my father. You can't fake the sound of your voice, particularly if you're too sick to care.'

Doctor Le Tissier was being very clever and using the odd phrase of patois to calm the tramp while he examined him.

'He obviously understands the patois,' whispered Basil. 'My father was very interested in the patois, he said it shouldn't be allowed to die. He was going to compile a dictionary . . . the war stopped all that . . .' Basil gripped my shoulder hard. He looked as if he was going to cry. There was a silence and then Doctor Le Tissier straightened up.

'I should like you to go to hospital immediately. Your body temperature is dangerously low, despite this young lady's splendid efforts. You need to be in a warm environment to regain normal temperature. If you stay here, to put it bluntly, you'll die.'

'I'm not going to hospital.'

'If it was just a question of getting warm again, you wouldn't need a hospital; any warm room would do the trick. But you're seriously ill as well. You *must* have hospital treatment, Mr . . . what is your name by the way?' Doctor Le Tissier asked the question casually as he put his stethoscope away. The silence lengthened until Basil suddenly rushed forward. He took the tramp's head between his hands and almost shook him as he shouted:

'You're Robert Le Patourel. I *know* you're Robert Le Patourel. Don't lie to us.'

'Who are you?' The tramp's eyes were shut; he looked almost like a corpse as he whispered these words.

'I'm your son, Basil, your bloody eldest son, remember?' shouted Basil. 'And at home, thinking you're dead, are my mother and Agnes and Marie and Pierre.' Basil was beside himself . . . rage, frustration, relief, even delight were in his voice. Tears were running down his face. 'Dad, Dad. Come back.'

'Basil. Bas. You've grown so tall.' Robert Le Patourel's eyes opened and met his son's. 'You don't want me home, I'm no use to any of you now.'

'Oh, God.' Basil wiped his tears with his sleeve and turned away. 'Just come back home Dad, we don't mind what state you're in.'

'He must go to hospital first.' Doctor Le Tissier was looking very confused. 'Are you really Robert Le Patourel?'

'Has Sophie kept my orchids alive?' The sick

man's face was almost transparent under its layer of dirt. His voice was a thread. 'I often thought of those orchids . . .' His face faded. For a dreadful moment I thought he'd died; Doctor Le Tissier leapt forward.

'He's lost consciousness. I'm going to rush down to the Imperial Hotel on the sea-front to telephone for an ambulance, then I'll come straight back. Hang on here for me.' He ran out.

The tramp's skin felt cold; I wrapped his limp hands round the cooling stone bottle and tucked the blankets tightly round his body.

'The old bastard.' Basil was grinning all over his face. 'The old bastard. Hiding on the island and none of us knew. Him and his goat, who'd have known him?'

'What's Aunt Sophie going to do when she hears?'

'She'll collapse.' Basil's grin faded. 'She'll feel strange, like I feel strange. Happy, but . . . well, angry too.'

'I'm going to get Daphne.'

I ran out of the bunker. I was afraid of the next few hours; I could see that the joy would be mixed with great pain. And there was also the fact that Robert Le Patourel was very ill; ill in his body, ill in his mind. Only someone very crazy would have behaved as he had since the end of the war. I could begin to sympathize with Basil's anger that he'd been living near them without revealing himself.

Daphne was eating busily and was not very willing to come with me. I picked a handful of grass to lure her on and led her towards the bunker. She skipped down the steps, bleating a couple of times.

I took her right up to the tramp's bed and she nuzzled his hand. After a while the tramp made a faint noise and tried to stroke Daphne's nose with his finger. He'd regained a faint thread of consciousness and all of it was concentrated on his goat.

'Daphne . . .' His breathing was terrible to hear.

'I'll look after her while you're in hospital. We'll take her back to Maison de Haut with us, won't we, Basil?'

Daphne nudged her master; she really seemed to sense that something was wrong. I don't know how intelligent goats are normally, but this one was like a dog.

'How are we going to get her back?' said Basil. 'I'm not putting a goat into Ted's car. She'd probably refuse to get in it, anyway.'

'I'll walk her back. I think I'll take her outside again,' I said to the tramp . . . I couldn't think of him as Robert Le Patourel, my uncle.

'No, please leave her.' I could hardly hear his voice.

So Daphne's hooves tapped round as she looked for things to eat. The cheese sandwiches disappeared in record time; then she started on one of Flo Guillemette's blankets.

'Bloody goat,' said Basil. 'I'm going up to see if Le Tissier is on his way back yet.' He pushed Daphne roughly away from the blanket as he passed her. I suppose he was resentful of the goat because his father was more interested in her than in his newly-found son.

When we were alone, I leaned close to the sick man and asked: 'What would you like me to do with your money?'

'The tin's out. Bring it here.' I fetched it and laid it beside him. 'I'll take it with me.'

'Or Basil could take care of it.'

Robert Le Patourel lay with his eyes shut, frowning. 'They'll open it,' he wheezed out at last.

'I'm sure they won't if you don't want them to.' I wondered if we'd ever find out why he trusted his family so little and why he'd hidden himself away. I stroked Daphne's harsh coat. It was a pity she couldn't talk.

38

The St John's Ambulance men took Robert Le Patourel away on a stretcher and Doctor Le Tissier followed the ambulance as it set off for the hospital. Basil and I stood desolate as they disappeared round the corner. Daphne wandered off into La Falaise to find more things to eat.

Then Basil decided to try to put Daphne into Ted's car after all, but she dug her heels in and would not move. He tried to lift her in and she bleated in terror.

'I'll have to walk her back, Bas.'

'Let's tie the wretched goat up and come back for her tomorrow.'

'I don't mind walking her back . . .'

'Come with me, Nancy. I can't face them on my own.' Basil suddenly crumpled against the car and began to weep. 'Doctor Le Tissier says Dad has tuberculosis and that he could be very near death. How am I going to break all this to Mum? The doctor says it's better not to hide the truth . . . he said not to give Mum too much hope that Dad will pull through because he doesn't think he will.'

'He could be wrong, Bas.'

'Yeah, he could be wrong. But I don't think he is and nor does he.' Basil's tears had ended as quickly as they'd begun and anger was coming back into his face. 'Nancy, why did the silly bugger hide himself away while he got sicker and sicker? It's too much to meet him again and find him like this.'

I didn't know what to say. As Daphne was heading out of the gate, I caught her and tied her up to a post in the overgrown orchard. I gave her some water and told her I'd be back for her tomorrow. Her yellow eyes were as expressionless as ever. I went back to Basil, who was sitting slumped in the driver's seat.

'Thank God it was you who came with me,' I said. 'If it had just been the doctor, we might never have found out who the tramp really was.'

'I'm beginning to think it would have been better that way,' said Basil hoarsely as he started the car.

39

The whole of that Saturday was a day I'll remember as long as I live. When Basil and I got back to the house it was still empty. I couldn't believe it was only four o'clock.

'Let's make some tea.'

We sat at the warm end of the large kitchen table sipping our tea. Neither of us was hungry. The cat sat on the draining-board and stared at us as if he found it strange that we should be sitting together in the middle of the afternoon, tensely waiting.

'How did you get to know Dad in the first place?' Basil broke the silence.

'I saw him on the cliff near La Falaise and we got talking. I'd already seen him before . . . He asked me for some aspirins one day and I took them to him. That was when he showed me his bunker, I think. He kept saying Nancy was a yankee name.'

'Did he know who you were? He could have linked you with the fact he had a niece called Nancy.'

'I'm sure he didn't. He didn't seem interested in the life around him at all. He was a lost soul.' I didn't really know what I meant by that, except that I knew I was right.

'Is a lost soul. We're talking about my father as if he's in the past.'

'The tramp part of him is in the past now. They'll clean him up in hospital. You'll see him as he really is.'

'You've been a bit of a lost soul yourself, Nancy. It must be hard for you here, on the edge of things.'

On the edge of things . . . but I wasn't any more. I could feel I'd been drawn in. My roots in Assam were being tugged at.

'Here they are.'

We heard the car stop and Aunt Sophie and Marie and Pierre walked in together, all in a very good humour. Their day had obviously gone well. I think it was the strength of their good mood that made Basil break the news the way he did.

'You won't believe the news we've got for you.

I can hardly believe it myself.' All three stopped, their smiles still in place. 'We've found Dad.' Then came the silence, the fading of the smiles into stunned surprise.

'What do you mean, found Dad?' said Marie at last. Aunt Sophie had gone white and was leaning against the back door.

'Go on,' she whispered. Basil stood tongue-tied. 'Go on.'

'A tramp with a goat.' Basil's lips began to quiver and he looked as if he might cry again. He took a deep breath. 'Nancy got to know him and today she found he'd collapsed. She took me along to help when the doctor came, and when I saw him I . . . I . . . It was Dad. They've taken him to hospital.'

'Oh, Basil, *Basil* . . .'

I knew I had to leave that kitchen; they needed to be alone. I slipped out unnoticed except by the cat who leapt off the draining-board and followed me upstairs.

On the edge of things . . . Sammy and I sat on my bed and I knew as I stroked his ears and listened to his thunderous purring, that whatever happened next, I'd be best away from Maison de Haut. If Robert Le Patourel survived they would bring him here to convalesce; they wouldn't want a spare person around. If he died, they still wouldn't want me around.

I heard the car start again and looked out of the window to see it disappear on its way to the hospital. I was alone in the house. I think they'd forgotten my existence and I wasn't surprised.

I lay on the bed, curled round the soundly-sleeping body of the cat, and tried to read *Lorna*

Doone. I couldn't concentrate and fell asleep for a while until the telephone jerked me awake. I ran downstairs in the dark and lifted the receiver off its hook on the wall. I stood on a stool to talk into the fixed mouthpiece.

'Hullo?'

'Grand-mère here. That's Nancy, isn't it?'

'Oh Granny . . .' I wailed.

'What on earth's the matter?'

'It's been such a strange, terrible day . . .' I poured everything out. She showed the same shock, joy and anger that Basil had done.

'Do you mean he's been on this island for months? I don't believe anyone could be so cruel to their family. He must be sick in mind as well as body. He was always very strange, to tell the truth. But very lovable too, great fun to be with if he was in a good mood.' My grandmother's voice was so warm and comforting in my ear that I didn't want the call to end. 'Nancy, my child, I'm going to come and get you, come and get you now. The last thing poor Sophie needs is an extra person to worry about at the moment. I'd like to see her anyway, so when I've told Aby everything, we'll both come over to Maison de Haut. How do you feel about staying here for a while?'

'Oh, Grand-mère.' I started to cry.

'You don't have to if you really don't want to; I was thinking of Sophie—'

'But I *do*! I was just thinking I couldn't stay here and wondering what on earth to do.'

'There, don't be a silly goat, you should have known you could come here. Start packing a few things, Nancy, and I'll explain everything to Sophie

215

myself when I come. Poor Sophie, poor love.'

I went up to my room again. The empty house creaked round me; all the internal walls and floors had a life of their own. The oak panels were as old as the house . . . three hundred years old and more. Maison de Haut was full that night of the presence of the people who'd lived there. The handmade metal latch to my room was worn smooth by all the hands that had pressed it down; three hundred years' worth of hands. I shivered.

'Mew.' The cat sat in the doorway watching me pack. He had a silly little mew for such a large cat. 'Mew.' I realized he was hungry and, when I'd finished putting my school things and a few clothes into a case, I followed him downstairs. Usually my aunt had a saucepan of horrid-smelling fish for him on the range, but today of course nothing was prepared. I looked in the larder and found the cat's saucepan on the stone floor. I spooned some of the cold fish heads and flesh into Sammy's dish and he fell on his food as if he hadn't been fed for a month. I felt fairly hungry myself now; all I'd had that day was bacon for breakfast and that hurried sandwich at the Guillemettes'. I ate a cold potato and a piece of cheese and drank some milk. 'Mew.' I gave Sammy some as well and he purred his appreciation.

I think if he hadn't been with me all evening, I'd have been frightened alone in that house.

My grandparents arrived five minutes before the others returned from the hospital. While everybody embraced and cried and talked and milled about, Basil took me aside.

216

'You've no idea how different he looks already. They've taken all his smelly clothes away and trimmed his hair and his beard and washed him. He looks like Dad again. Old, thin, sick, but Dad again. It's amazing how all that matted hair disguised him. And his clothes too, of course.'

'Was he angry at being in hospital?'

'He was hardly conscious, too weak to be angry. That'll no doubt come later! But even though he was so weak, he knew everyone. He held our hands and tears came out of his eyes.' Basil hugged me suddenly. 'We're so grateful to you, Nancy.'

Aunt Sophie came over to me too and grabbed me. 'Nancy, Nancy, if you hadn't been kind to a tramp, we'd never have found him. He would have died in that bunker within a day or two, Doctor Le Tissier said. We'd have never known it was him. It doesn't bear thinking about.' She crushed me against her rough tweed coat; I could feel her tears dropping on my forehead.

Agnes leaned over her mother and kissed my cheek and whispered: 'Thanks, kid.'

Then Marie and Pierre came and kissed me too and in a way that meant more than anything. I cried, everyone was crying. Then we all started to laugh when Basil added:

'The one thing we mustn't do is forget that bloody goat! Dad'll never forgive us. What's her name, Nancy?'

'Daphne.'

'Daphne. If she's here when he comes out of hospital he won't mind that all his orchids are dead.'

My aunt blew her nose and wiped her tears away. 'Time to eat something,' she said.

NOVEMBER 1949

I can't believe that it's tomorrow. I really can't. I keep looking out of my window at the Little Russel and watching the boats going to and from Herm, or Sark, or Jersey. Tomorrow the mail-boat will arrive and on it will be my parents and Clare and Robert.

My grandparents gave me Abraham's room, the long attic at the top of the house. It's like having a flat of my own; there's a little kitchen and a bathroom, as well as the big main room with its dormer windows and one long window on the end wall with a little balcony and the most wonderful view. Every morning I make my own breakfast – I go to school before my grandparents leave their bedroom – and if it's fine I sit out and eat it staring at all the islands: Herm, Jethou, Brecqhou, Sark and away to the left Alderney, which, like Jersey and the coast of France, is only visible on a clear day.

Today has the sort of clarity I remember in Assam in the cold weather. Absolute stillness and an intense blue sky and clear, clear air. The only difference as usual is in what I can smell: instead of all those peculiarly Indian scents I breathe in salt wind and sea and bonfires and frying bacon from the kitchen downstairs. It's Sunday. On Sundays I have a late breakfast after church with my grand-parents; not that I always go to church with them. I heard them come back about ten minutes ago and soon they'll be ringing the gong for me. One bang with the mallet means come now, two means in five minutes and three means there's someone on the telephone or at the door for me. We've got our lives very well worked out.

When I look at the Nancy who came to live here not long before Christmas two years ago, I can hardly believe she and I are the same person. She seemed to be climbing out of a cave of her own making and I've been running in the air ever since. She was still trying to hold on to the past and I've let it go.

When Uncle Robert died Guernsey was blanketed in snow; 1947-8 was the worst winter for ages. I remember how my grandparents' car slithered about as we drove through the snow-banked lanes to be with Aunt Sophie when she telephoned us to say the end was near. Everyone said we'd never get to St Peters in the Wood but Grand-père had put chains on the car wheels and we managed somehow, though twice we skidded right into the bank.

Uncle Robert looked so young and peaceful at the end; he died with a smile on his face and his curly hair was soft and sweet-smelling on the pillow. I kissed his cold cheek; I felt a wave of gratitude towards him, though precisely why I couldn't have said because I didn't know. I found myself saying his poem silently as I looked at him. I'd learned it by heart when I'd discovered it was a song sung by Ariel in *The Tempest*.

> Nothing of him that doth fade,
> But doth suffer a sea change
> Into something rich and strange.

It's such a warm day for November; I've been sitting out on my balcony and even now the windows are wide open. I look round this lovely room; there on the mantelpiece is Abraham's mechanical tiger, still broken – I confessed to Grand-mère I had done it – but still splendidly fierce with his frozen growl.

All my friends love this room and being so near the college, they pop in for half an hour on the way home any day. Stella comes nearly every day and so does her cousin Andrew. Andrew came into my life last year . . . but that's another story.

There's a yacht in full sail moving slowly towards Jersey, very slowly because there isn't much wind. Jersey looks almost as if it has a small range of mountains because of a low bank of pinkish cloud beyond the island . . . pink mountains . . .

Oh, those deliciously cool-looking peaks away across the Assam Valley, mountains crowned with icing, sometimes blue, sometimes pink, sometimes white. And those four great pinnacles edging higher into the sky, Chen, Kangdu, Chumo, Nyegi Kainsang. Names I could never forget, names I still chant when I'm lying in bed, trying to get to sleep. Chen, Kangdu, Chumo, Nyegi Kainsang. Oh Himalayas, you are so far away, so far out of my life now. But you'll never be out of my being. I will get to Assam again one day, I will gaze across at you from the Shillong Peak and I'll sing your silent icy beauty again as I ride away down through those resiny pine-woods . . . Oh Himalayas . . .

I hear the gong sound twice. I shut my long window and as I do so I stare at the Little Russel as if that mail-boat is going to appear any minute and start its big curve into St Peter Port harbour. I can't wait to see them again, those shadowy figures who lie closest to my heart, to see my parents, to see Clare transformed into a four-year-old and to pick up and hug my new brother Robert. I haven't even seen a photograph of him yet; he's only three months old. I'll pick him up and hold him against my shoulder as Congreeal used to hold us and I'll pat his back and sing, just as she did:

> *Nini baba nini,*
> *Roti makhan cini*
> *Roti makhan ho-gya*
> *Nini baba so-gya.*